A Domestic Affair

For Colin Fletcher, estate agent, the misery of divorce was as bad as that of marriage. Not only was his ex-wife a financial drain on him, but she persistently obstructed his legal right of access to their two children. But if he could prove her an unfit person to have control of them, the case would be altered. Fletcher engaged a private investigator to watch his wife.

At first fate seemed to be playing into his hands. Louise inserted an advertisement for suitable companionship in a local paper, and very soon a wealthy companion turned up. When Fletcher and a woman witness arrived at the house late one evening to find that Louise had not come home to her children, it looked as though Fletcher had the evidence he sought.

Unfortunately his ex-wife's disappearance posed more problems than it solved, one of them — and potentially the most serious — being created by Louise herself. Then the private investigator, though sacked by Fletcher, insisted on involving the police. Even the children unexpectedly took a hand in the solution to this ingenious domestic mystery which is both startling and original.

by the same author

THE SEARCH FOR SARA
ALL PART OF THE SERVICE
RAINBLAST
BACKLASH
CATSPAW
DEATH FUSE
TOUCHDOWN
A DANGEROUS PLACE TO DWELL
DAYLIGHT ROBBERY
DIAL DEATH
MR T
DOUBLE DEAL
MURDER BY THE MILE
THE CLIENT
PHANTOM HOLIDAY
CRIME WAVE
DOUBLE HIT
CONCRETE EVIDENCE
ADVISORY SERVICE
DEADLINE
HUNT TO A KILL
DANGER MONEY
NO RETURN TICKET
NO THROUGH ROAD

MARTIN RUSSELL

A Domestic Affair

COLLINS, 8 GRAFTON STREET, LONDON W1

William Collins Sons & Co. Ltd
London · Glasgow · Sydney · Auckland
Toronto · Johannesburg

First published 1984

British Library Cataloguing in Publication Data

Russell, Martin
A domestic affair.—(Crime Club).
I. Title
823′.914[F]   PR6068.U86

ISBN 0 00 231386 3

Photoset in Compugraphic Baskerville
by T. J. Press (Padstow) Ltd
Printed in Great Britain by
William Collins Sons & Co. Ltd, Glasgow

CHAPTER 1

'Before we get down to cases,' said the dark-haired man, 'let me offer a guarantee. I'm not wired for sound. There's no video-cassette taped to my midriff. I've not planted a bug under the—'

'What makes you think it would concern me if you had?'

The man looked disconcerted. 'Generally speaking, people in your position—'

'My position?'

'No offence, Mr Fletcher. In this job, there are certain assumptions one tends to make. Not always justified.'

'The same might be true in reverse.'

The dark-haired man pondered for a moment. Movements of a hand suggested that he was about to rotate the coffee in his cup, but it came to nothing. Fletcher studied the hand. Thick-fingered, hairless, with cropped nails, it carried hints of arthritic swellings at the joints. A draught from the coffee-bar door made a sneak attack at knee-level. The man slid closer to the wall, jerked at his leather topcoat.

'You've reservations about me?'

'I'm reserved by nature, Mr Ferrari. We've only just met.' Sipping from his own cup, Fletcher kept his gaze attached to the other's slightly careworn, fiftyish face. 'I notice you've not asked me if *I'm* wired for sound. You'd regard that as an occupational hazard?'

'Depends what we're going to be discussing.'

'Nothing treasonable, I can assure you.'

Ferrari looked across at the service counter, where the girl running it was using a vivid yellow sponge to wipe down the refinery piping that towered between her and the customers. Having devoted a period of brooding attention to her activities, he said meditatively, 'We could keep this up all night. Time's money to me, Mr Fletcher.'

'I'll come to the point in a minute. I like to try and get to know the people I deal with.'

Ferrari glanced back at him. 'If you're that choosy, I'd have thought you might have gone to one of the bigger outfits, like Henderson's. Why me? I rely on Press ads for my custom and I don't even have an office.'

'Henderson's are out of range of my pocket. I asked. Besides which, they didn't show much enthusiasm for a mere domestic case. Industrial espionage is probably more in their line.'

Inhaling a sip of coffee, Ferrari brooded again. 'Your wife comes into this?'

'My ex.' Fletcher snapped a ginger biscuit, guided half into his mouth.

'She's getting demanding?' Ferrari hypothesized.

'She was always that. I used to think she was just about worth it.'

'Only now that you're split . . .'

'I don't see why I should be regarded as her meal-ticket for life.'

'They all say that.'

'The voice of broad experience,' Fletcher said sourly. 'All right: it's a trite situation, I know. Aren't most of them? Money, jealousy, revenge . . .'

'The situations are basic. It's the variations on them that make the difference.'

Fletcher retired into reflection. Presently he shifted, rearranging himself sideways on an elbow, his shoulder in contact with the flock-papered wall. 'To hell with it. Even if you decide against taking the case, it'll be a relief just to tell someone other than a legal zombie. I hope you're a good listener.'

*

Before we married, Louise was a travel agent. Her description, not mine. She did work in an agency, but as a small cog in a sizeable, multi-faceted dream machine, helping people to plan the quickest way to spend their life savings on world cruises. She had enjoyed the job. She never tired of telling me how much she had liked it, the implication being that nothing since then had been remotely comparable, that she had renounced a kingdom for a croft. Looking back, I marvel at her ever having consented to relinquish the post. For my sake? I doubt it.

For a few years I served a purpose. Having provided her with a family, I was needed for its material support and so my presence in the house was tolerated. Where? Here in Bancester—that is, just outside, on the eastbound road to Oxford. Noisy at peak times, but undeniably handy for shops and transport and other essentials. Since it's a detached place with nine rooms, the upkeep is something of a drain, but up until the divorce I could just about cope.

I'm an estate agent. Well, as in Louise's case, that may be something of a euphemism: I work, shall we say, in the branch office of an estate agency based in Abingmore, my function being to supply the clerical back-up to those engaged in actually selling the property, and my salary being fixed, with nil chances of commission. Don't imagine I'm complaining. I never saw myself as a salesman, and ordinarily I'd be only too thankful to have a secure job in a time of recession: I don't aim high. All I ask is a fair crack of the whip.

Maybe my outlook is dull. I wouldn't know. To someone like Louise, I dare say I rank as a plodder, deficient in charisma. If so, it could account for her eventual conclusion that the strain of putting up with me was no longer worth enduring, as well as for her dedication in pursuing the task of ditching the burden.

Her methods were traditional and uncomplicated.

First, the assiduous undermining; finally, the cluster of karate chops. When it came to picking a quarrel, Louise came ready-armed with all the devices of her sex, plus a few extras she had equipped herself with en route. One disagreement in particular sticks in my mind.

How it arose, I have very little idea. At some point, with dismal inevitability, finance crept into the argument, and it was at this juncture that Louise committed the unpardonable crime: she hauled Terri—the small daughter I had helped to produce—into our tension-packed bedroom to demonstrate the supposedly threadbare condition of her school blazer. 'See this?' I recall her demanding, clasping Terri with one hand while she wrenched at the fabric with the other. 'Having your children go about in rags doesn't seem to bother you. Well, it bothers me. What do you intend doing about it?'

For Terri's sake I kept a tight rein on my temper. 'I thought you were going to buy her a new one?'

'What am I supposed to use for cash?'

'Surely I give you enough to—'

'Kids' clothing costs a bomb. Did no one ever tell you?'

I made the mistake of addressing Terri directly. 'Sure that's the only blazer you have, darling? I had the impression—'

'Are you calling me a liar, or what?' Louise's voice was low and perilous. 'I've told you. She needs a new outfit. I'm not looking for a fight. I'm simply stating the obvious. Why make an issue of it every time?'

On another occasion I could scarcely have avoided reacting to this. The reason that I didn't, this time, was Terri herself. Making no attempt to reply to my question, she merely looked at me with empty eyes before turning away to finger the cosmetics on her mother's dressing-table, presenting to me a small and seemingly hostile back which left me stripped of words. Sick at stomach,

I turned and left the room.

Later, I left thirty pounds in cash under the cold cream jar on the dressing-table. Later still, it vanished. Nothing more was said; I couldn't make out whether Terri acquired a new blazer or not; things went on as before, a cold war unbroken by peace overtures. Like many women, Louise could maintain an antagonistic silence without apparent difficulty for as long as it took, and in my case it wasn't long. After the blazer bust-up, I knew it was the finish. If I had lost the affection and respect of a seven-year-old daughter—to say nothing of a nine-year-old son—there was little to be gained by repeatedly gloss-painting the façade of our domestic structure: better to acknowledge the yawning cracks and kick it down. Within a year of my leaving the house, Louise and I were divorced. But that was just the start of my problems.

'You don't need to tell me all this,' Ferrari said morosely. 'An outline would have done.'

'I want you to have the full picture,' Fletcher explained. 'I'd prefer it that way.'

'Is it me you're trying to convince? Or yourself?'

'Now look,' Fletcher said vexedly. 'I'm not looking for sermons . . . is that understood? I've taken enough stick to last me a lifetime. All I'm giving you is the balance-sheet. On that basis, it's for you to decide whether or not to take up the option. Fair enough?'

The dark-haired private investigator surveyed his coffee cup, then gave a single jerk of the head. 'Carry on,' he sighed.

Predictably, Louise was given custody of the children and she also kept the house. My side of the bargain was to provide the living expenses.

For the first few weeks I had the use of a converted flat which came on to the books of the estate agency. When that sold, I managed to obtain the tenancy of an old, detached cottage a mile or two outside the village of Stroudbury, south of Abingmore, pending its disposal by the executors of the aged female who had dwelt in it for the previous sixty years. My occupancy was hedged around with enough restrictive clauses to paper a ceiling: I could never feel secure for more than a month ahead at a time, but since my immediate future had no particular shape to it, that aspect concerned me only slightly. My chief worry lay elsewhere.

Under the terms of the divorce settlement, I had been granted 'reasonable access' to the children. Precisely what was reasonable or otherwise seemed, as always, to have been left to the parties involved to decide. Which in practice meant that it was Louise who decided. Which, in turn, meant that in a breathtakingly brief space of time I found myself effectively frozen out. After the initial weekend, when I took a pair of faintly perplexed and pronouncedly withdrawn youngsters to a safari park and a cinema, bought them tea and tried without noticeable success to converse with them, my path to their door turned out to be mined with booby-traps that exploded one by one beneath my feet. Telephone appeals to Louise were inclined to backfire.

'Well, if Kevin's feeling under the weather, can't I take Terri by herself?'

'You know perfectly well they like to do everything together. If Terri went without him, he'd be terribly upset.'

'Surely she can just come over and spend the evening with me? We can watch TV.'

'They've already made plans to play *Hazard*. I'm not having either of them forced to disrupt their arrangements, it's unsettling. You'll have to wait until next week.'

Next week, it was Terri who had 'caught the bug' from

Kevin. The week after, both of them had gone off on a school trip to Wales—'And by the way, it's costing twenty-five quid each, so you'd better let me have a cheque by Monday because I had to take it out of the allowance.' The week after that . . .

I forget the details. All that I remember is the resourcefulness, the sheer ingenuity of Louise in keeping me at a distance, sanitarily quarantined. I consulted my solicitor, who advised me to seek an injunction. Not liking the sound of that, I withheld Louise's maintenance for a month, and immediately she took out an injunction against me. To fight it would have meant further expenditure. I could have ignored it, challenged her to take supplementary action, risked imprisonment. I could have taken my lawyer's advice, tried to vindicate myself in court with counter-accusations of access denial. All extremely messy, and harmful to the children. Their interests remained paramount. I sent Louise the money.

Four of us worked in my office at the estate agency. One was a part-timer, a woman whose job was to type and duplicate details of properties on the firm's headed sheets. Her name was Eva Maynard. Still in her early thirties, she was a widow: her husband, we understood, had died in an industrial mishap a year or so previously. The tragedy seemed to have left its mark. Her tight, almost sullen features gave the impression of being fenced in, boxed off, keeping her unreachable at her desk as she prodded, brisk and accurate, at the keyboard of her machine. Her figure was small and neat. With a little attention, her coppery hair could have been striking instead of hung about her head, as it was, like bundles of fuse-wire. When I had to address her, I called her Mrs Maynard. She called me Mr Fletcher.

Between her desk and mine sat two younger girls, Polly and Irene. Giggling and confiding their way through each seven-hour working stretch, they treated both of us with the amicable indifference of a separate generation, for all that the age-gap was no more than a decade. Medium-sized though the office was, my isolation by the window was complete.

One morning, when both girls were out for their coffee break and Eva Maynard was tapping away as obliviously as usual, a call came through from Louise.

'The cheque hasn't arrived.' She was never one to waste time on preliminaries. 'You're not messing me around again?'

'I sent it off on the twenty-eighth,' I told her, 'You should have had it by the thirtieth.'

'Today's the third and there's no sign of it.'

'Obviously it's gone astray. I'll cancel that one and send you another. Louise, while you're on . . .'

'Do it today, will you? I'm very short.'

'I must put a stop on the other cheque first. You'll have to wait a day or two, I'm afraid. Don't panic, you'll get it.'

'That's easy to say. You don't have to cater for a family. I've bills coming in the whole time. How do you imagine I—'

'I do have expenses of my own,' I said, in an undertone but very distinctly. 'I'm not entirely removed from material problems, it may astound you to know. But I'll keep my end of the bargain, don't worry . . . provided you make some sort of gesture towards keeping yours.' I lowered my voice further. 'When can I see them, Louise? It's been more than two months. I'm supposed to have weekly access, for God's sake. Unless they—'

'*Reasonable* access. Nothing was said about every week.'

'You consider four times a year to be reasonable?'

'You always were one to dramatize.' Her voice was remote. 'I'm the one looking after them, remember. I'll decide when they can cope with the mental disturbance of seeing someone they've had to learn to do without.

They're not to be upset. The doctor—'

'*Had to learn to do without?*' Inadvertently my voice climbed a notch or two. I turned my face to the window. 'There was never any question of such a thing, and you know it. Had they been allowed to see me, as arranged . . .'

'I'm not going to argue on the phone. Send the cheque, Colin, and leave the child guidance to me. If I don't get it within the next two days, there'll be trouble.' The phone went down.

Slowly I replaced the receiver. My index finger hovered above the dial while I debated a course of action, returned to the desk-top as I rejected it. Telephones were useless. With Louise, face-to-face confrontations were tricky enough: at a distance, unseen, untouchable, she could run rings around me. I felt weary, furious, desolate, impotent. Seven miles away, my children were growing up as strangers and there was apparently nothing I could do about it. Except pay out most of my income to perpetuate the process. Suddenly I couldn't see a future.

Turning back to my desk, I caught the eye of Eva Maynard. From the core of her intangible stockade she was regarding me as though seeking inspiration for a phrase. As my own gaze stabilized, hers returned to the sheet in her machine: she stabbed a word or two before wrenching out the finished product to compare it with the draft she had been given. My feeling was that she had been on the verge of saying something but had decided against it. Shortly afterwards the girls came back in a cloudburst of chatter, and distance re-established itself.

During the rest of that day I fretted over the situation. I could see not a chink of light. Each of the two courses open to me was as bad as the other. By taking legal action, I might reaffirm my status in the eyes of the law, but the practical outcome would be a minus factor: Louise would simply invent more insidious ways of keeping us all apart, and I couldn't keep taking her to court for ever. If, on the other hand, I were to write off the entire mess . . .

The notion of turning on my heel and sneaking away was repugnant. When all was said and done, I remained the father of Kevin and Terri. I had helped bring them into the world and I was damned if, having done so, I was going to leave meekly to Louise all the fun and fulfillment of bringing them up. Tied to a single parent, the pair of them would forfeit something of inestimable worth—and all because I had been too spineless to assert my rights.

But then, again, in striving to recapture those rights . . .

By the end of the day I felt mentally drained and no closer to a solution. At intervals I must have handled telephone queries, dictated letters: my memory was a blank. Polly and Irene left punctually at five. Twenty minutes later I hung up on the last caller and steered the line back to the switchboard before collecting my coat from its hook and bidding Eva Maynard good night. Normally she would have left at lunch-time, but on this occasion she had been asked to work overtime. As I reached the door, she halted her assault upon the keys and swivelled her chair.

'Mr Fletcher . . .'

'Yes?' I guessed she had a query about a price. I hoped it would keep. My one desire was to get out, away, to continue my mental wrestling without distraction.

'Do forgive me,' she said hesitantly, 'for asking you this, but . . . did I hear you talking to your wife earlier?'

'My ex-wife,' I confirmed tersely.

'Your ex. Sorry. I couldn't help overhearing.'

'No, of course not. I hope you weren't embarrassed.'

'Not a bit. I was angry.'

I felt myself blink. 'I beg your pardon?'

Rising, she came across to where I stood. 'I believe I picked up the gist of what was going on between you, and it got my blood up. She's keeping you from your children—is that it?'

'I dare say it must have been obvious.' My tone of voice was, I hoped, a warning and a deterrent. 'Thanks for getting worked up on my behalf.' I gave her a brief grin that was supposed to carry me through the doorway and out of sight, but it didn't. She put out a restraining hand.

'I was wondering if you might appreciate a spot of advice. My brother, you see . . . he went through a similar thing, actually. So I know quite a lot about it. Would it help to talk it over with someone?'

'It's very good of you,' I started to say, and then stopped. The brush-off had died unexpectedly on my lips. She was looking at me, not with the avid compassion of the soulmate-seeker but with the impersonal attentiveness of the consultant. It was the type of contact I urgently needed, and in contrast to my solicitor she was prepared to provide it, presumably, for the price of a meal, apart from being easier on the eye. 'It might help a lot,' I replied instead. 'Only I'd hate to impose. I'm sure you . . .'

The glance she gave me was, in an obscure way, eloquent. 'I can shelve my more pressing engagements,' she said drily.

Over a table, I recounted as much of the story as I deemed necessary, doing my utmost to present it fairly. Possibly I overdid it. The character of Louise emerged, I suspected, in a more favourable light than it merited, although Eva Maynard neither made nor signified any comment. Midway through the narrative, when she interpolated a question, I called her Eva. A little later she asked if she might use my first name, which meant that by the end of the first course we were on the sort of terms that in a comparable work-situation elsewhere might have been taken for granted months earlier. The curious formality that had grown up between us was not going to disintegrate overnight, but at least we had made a start.

Eva was a good listener. So good, that several times I lost the thread of my discourse by paying too much attention to the set of her mouth under the amber-shaded lighting of the restaurant. She looked more relaxed than I had ever seen her, and oddly enough a little older than usual . . . but in a pleasing way, as though a sudden maturity had rounded her features, softened her demeanour. The stockade had all but vanished. After I had brought her up to date she sat in silence for a minute or two, taking reflective sips of the house wine and seeming to observe the rather boisterous activities of a group at a nearby table. For my part I sat back, feeling easier now that I had unburdened myself, content for the moment simply to appreciate her company, not anticipating more from the evening than that. Presently she brought her gaze back to me.

'If I were offering you professional advice,' she said, 'it would probably run along these lines . . .'

What she proceeded to tell me could have come straight from the booming larynx of my lawyer: from her, it sounded marginally less obnoxious, that was all. I listened politely, nodded my head a few times, made assenting noises. I was relating what she said to the attitude of Louise, noting the flaws in the equation. Eva stopped talking, contemplated me for a space, then resumed on a different note.

'That's what the law says you should be doing. From what you've said, though, I doubt if it would get you anywhere. Would you like to examine the problem from a new slant?'

Ferrari stirred with more than a hint of restlessness. 'You're eating time,' he complained. 'Most of this I could have assumed for myself. What purpose—'

'If you're going to do a job for me,' said Fletcher, 'you're entitled to the fullest briefing I can give.'

'*If* I do a job for you.'

'It's your decision. I'm just doing my best to lay things squarely before you.'

The private investigator cogitated. 'In the normal way,' he said eventually, 'my clients tend to keep the background stuff to a minimum. What mostly concerns them is fixing a price.'

'And what is it that mostly concerns you?'

A shrug came over the table. 'I'm in the trade for a living. *No assignment too small to consider*,' Ferrari quoted helpfully. 'The ad doesn't say that for nothing, you know.'

CHAPTER 2

Reversing her Samba hatchback from the pencil-slim garage that went with her one-bedroomed flat on the fringes of Abingmore, Eva Maynard swung out into the main road and set course for Stroudbury. Safely past the first T-junction, she switched on the radio.

Mozart's 'Jupiter' Symphony was just commencing. The third movement was into its closing bars when she pulled up alongside a blackthorn hedge in a quiet, coal-black lane on the farther side of the village and flashed her headlamps. A few seconds elapsed. On the point of releasing her seat-belt, she stayed where she was as a figure emerged from a ragged gap in the hedge and came round to the passenger side. She leaned across to unlock the door. The figure opened it, ducked inside.

'Saw you arrive,' he apologized, 'but I had trouble locking the kitchen door. Needs oiling. I didn't want you to come knocking for me. What with the rain and then the frost, the crazy paving has gone berserk. Dicey in the dark.' He sat motionless, peering at her.

The glow from the dashboard was just enough to outline their faces. Eva said, 'You certainly don't indulge yourselves with street lighting around here.'

'I don't mind the dark. Sometimes.'

They sat in silence. Eva's hands were on the wheel. Turning in his seat, Fletcher inclined himself towards her, not quite touching. He stayed in that position. After a moment she removed her left hand from the wheel, put it around the back of his neck.

She pulled him gently forward until their cheeks were in contact. His skin smelt of soap and aftershave, hers of perfume. Slipping the seat-harness, she brought her right hand over to join the left one at his nape. For an instant he responded, then drew back. He murmured something.

She said, 'What?'

'I said, I still feel I should be the one calling for you in a car.'

'Just male touchiness. Anyway you don't have a car.'

'I did have. She's got it now.'

'Like everything else.'

'She needs it, with the children.'

'Naturally,' Eva said without expression.

Fletcher rested an elbow against the back of his seat, used his palm to support his face. 'That,' he said, 'was rather nice.'

'Sounds like a compliment to the chef.'

'Which reminds me—I'm starved. You?'

'I suppose I could be. Where are we eating?'

Settling back, he strapped himself in. 'Follow my directions,' he said mysteriously.

The rain spurted again, bringing down more dead twigs to clutter the windscreen. They were too much for the wipers. Switching off, Eva re-settled her head against his shoulder, reclaimed possession of his hand. 'Remind me,' she said drowsily, 'to get out and clear them before we move off.'

'We ought to be going.'

'Why?'

Fletcher reflected. 'I've no idea,' he confessed. 'It's a meaningless platitude. If we like it here, why the hell should we leave?'

'Mike would never have said that.'

'Restless type, was he?'

'Different from you,' she said, after a pause. 'Totally different. I'd never have dreamt . . .'

'What?'

'Forget it. What a super meal that was. We must go there again.'

'My last visit,' remarked Fletcher, 'was four years ago. I was afraid it might have changed.'

'Did you go there with her?'

'Uh-huh.'

'I hope she appreciated it.'

'Anything of that kind appeals to Louise.'

After another silence Eva said, 'You could try making her an offer.'

'Buy them back from her? If I thought she'd do it, I'd make a bid, if I had the cash.'

'But in the real world,' Eva continued, sitting up straighter and frowning at the dashboard light of the radio, which was tuned softly to a station pumping out Gershwin, 'strategems like that are non-starters. From what you've told me of Louise, if she was bleeding you for five million a year she'd still want the kids as well, if only to spite you.'

'As to her motives,' Fletcher said slowly, 'I wouldn't know. There could be an element of malice. But mainly, I think, she just takes it for granted she's the one who should have them. Most mothers feel that way, don't they?'

'You're very charitable.'

'Don't be fooled. My feelings towards Louise at this time would hardly bear inspection. I have to try to see things from her standpoint, if only to keep a sense of proportion.'

Leaning forward, Eva doused the radio. She turned to face him. 'Worried sick about them, aren't you?'

'If I weren't, would I have taken the steps I have already?'

Her smile was affectionate. 'From what I know of you, I'd say not. You think this man Ferrari is likely to get results?'

Fletcher shrugged. 'He says he's working to a plan. He's been on it now for two weeks, so it had better be good.'

'What's he charging?'

'It's partly cash on delivery. If he pulls it off, I give him a couple of hundred in addition to his daily rate.'

'What exactly is he hoping to *pull off?*'

'He's aiming,' Fletcher said reluctantly, 'to collect evidence to show that Louise isn't a fit person to have charge of a pair of youngsters. If he does, we can take it from there.'

'Think he stands any chance?'

'Your guess is as good as mine.'

'What sort of evidence?'

Fletcher scratched his scalp. 'Failing to look after them properly, I suppose. Any kind of neglect. I haven't pressed him for details.'

'Is Louise that type of mother?'

'Strictly speaking, no. As far as material welfare is concerned, she'd be conscientious. At a moral level . . .'

'You've said you don't think she's inclined to run after men.'

'I didn't quite say that. She's not sexually promiscuous, it's true. I'm certain of that. What I do believe is, she could be quite interested in teaming up with anyone she felt might . . . advance her prospects in some way. In fact . . .'

'In fact, what?' Eva prompted, as he paused.

'I've reason to believe she may have taken steps in that direction already. Do you read the personal columns?'

'In the *Gleaner*, you mean? Not unless I'm desperate for diversion.'

'I skim them sometimes. They can be entertaining. There's an ad in this week which caught my eye.'

'Why?'

'Just the style it was worded. I'm almost sure it was Louise.'

'Advertising for companionship, you mean? How ghastly.'

'She wouldn't see it that way. There's a certain down-to-earth directness about Louise. She approves of modern methods. If she felt lonely, she wouldn't sit there stewing, she'd do something about it. The reason I think it's her, the ad mentions *friendship without frills*. That's a phrase she's used before. I could be quite wrong, of course.'

'It's quite likely you are. There must be dozens of other women in the district who . . .' Eva was silent for a moment, staring into the darkness beyond the windscreen. 'Getting back to Ferrari. Have you got faith in him?'

Fletcher's shoulders moved again. 'Unless and until he achieves something, how is one to know?'

Eva tapped the wheel with her fingernails. 'It all seems rather unsatisfactory.'

He gave a short laugh. 'As an understatement, that qualifies for a gold medallion. What else do you suggest?'

'I've offered my suggestion.'

'I didn't think you were serious.' He studied her through the gloom.

'Where children are concerned, I'm always serious.'

Fletcher allowed a moment or two to pass. 'You and

Mike never tried for a family, I assume?'

'You assume wrong.' Her voice had recaptured the flatness it had always possessed in the office, before they got acquainted.

'No luck?'

'Luck didn't come into it. I can't have children.'

'I see.' His embarrassment showed. 'You're sure about that? Sometimes it's the man who—'

'We both had all the tests. It's me, I'm afraid. Not quite . . . complete.' She turned her head to look blindly through the side window.

'You're fond of youngsters, though?' Fletcher said presently.

She remained still. 'To have a family I could call my own . . . I'd give almost anything in the world.'

CHAPTER 3

The Farmhouse Tearoom in the centre of Bancester was famous for its home-baked scones. Neither Louise nor her friend Sally could resist them. For a skin-blistering March morning they were especially suitable, plastered with creamy butter and chased by gulps of the home-ground coffee for which the Farmhouse was likewise esteemed. The indulgence had become almost a daily practice with the two of them. Sally still worked part-time at the travel agency near by, and Louise had small difficulty in finding a reason most mornings to drive her Datsun the two miles into the Market Square for shopping and a chat. They liked and understood one another.

'I tell you, Sal, the whole thing's starting to get to me.'

Sally Wentworth gave a slow, sympathetic nod. A square-faced woman in her forties, she had long since abandoned hope of—or indeed an urge for—a romantic life of her own, and she valued her association with someone younger, more glamorous, more extrovert who was more than willing to confide. It made a welcome change from being a captive listener to the prattle of her housebound mother, who everyone said was 'incredibly good' for her age, but whose horizons inevitably were limited.

'I can understand,' she said, 'how you feel.'

'He's so tight-fisted—it's not true. Can you guess what his pitch is, this month? The cheque's got lost in the post! Even his excuses are dull. He makes me want to scream.'

'I'm sure he does.'

'There he sits, coining the loot on the property market and splurging half of it on himself, while here am I at home with the kids, scratching around for things to feed and clothe them with, waiting patiently for money that never . . .'

'It's too bad.' Offering her friend a light for the cigarette she had wrestled out of her handbag, Sally drew the bill for the coffee and scones covertly towards her own plate. 'I've never met Colin, but he sounds as if he wants locking up.'

Louise regarded her cynically through clouds of smoke. 'What good would that do? I'd be more stuck for cash than ever. While he's at large, I can at least pile the pressure on.'

'But it's so wearing for you.'

'Never get married, Sal. Then you'll escape divorce.'

Sally smiled, a shade ruefully. 'Despite everything, how are the children?'

'In rude spirits. Kevin seems to want to go into computers.'

'I hope he manages to get out. Terri?'

'Has leanings towards the ballet. She affirms.' Louise knocked ash into her saucer. 'Do schools study the wishes of pupils these days? They never did in mine.'

'From what you read, or see on television, they're chiefly obsessed with teaching them about sex.'

'Yes. I can't decide whether they're responding to the new liberal climate or busily helping to create it. You have to be terrified for juveniles at times. Terri mentioned a man only yesterday.'

'Oh no?'

'It's all right, apparently he didn't do anything. She just happened to notice him when she was coming out of school. He was in a car, parked a little way along. Just sitting there, watching.'

'Waiting for a child of his own, perhaps?'

Louise shook her head. 'Terri thought not. As she was climbing into the bus she glanced back and saw him drive off—by himself.'

'That doesn't prove anything.'

'Granted . . . but he'd done the same thing the previous day. Terri spotted him both times.'

Sally looked grave. 'Have you mentioned it to her teacher?'

'Phoned her this morning. She seemed inclined to play it down, but she did promise to see the children personally on to the bus in future—and she also said she'd mention it to the police. I didn't say anything to discourage her. One can't be too cautious.'

'I suppose . . .' Sally frowned into her coffee cup. 'You're quite happy about the school bus itself? What about the driver? Has he been properly vetted?'

A snort of laughter came from Louise. 'In the States,' she observed, 'that query would be taken in a more medical sense than you mean. The bus driver, my dear, is above suspicion, one would hope. She's a woman.'

'Oh. That's sensible. Such a pity to entertain these ideas, especially in a quiet town like this, but what's the choice? No use being sorry afterwards.'

'*Quiet*,' echoed Louise, after a pause, 'is the word that

fits. You never spoke truer, Sally my pet. Tell me something. Do you ever feel like standing on top of the Corn Exchange dressed as a Red Indian, shrieking at the top of your voice and brandishing a tomahawk?'

'It's not one of my fantasies,' Sally said cautiously. 'Is that how you feel sometimes?'

'Not often. Only every evening, around six.'

Sally studied her friend compassionately. 'You're lonesome.'

Leaning back in her chair, Louise gazed unseeingly across the tearoom at the chintz curtains over the diamond-paned windows. 'As far as men are concerned, as a breed,' she announced finally, 'I've never regarded myself as a besotted disciple. Less than ever, since Colin and I split. By and large, I can take 'em or leave 'em. One has to admit it, though . . . just now and again, a better sample of the species can add a touch of spice to the odd hour. Even if it's only as someone to take things out on. They're quite good for that, poor lambs.'

'Louise, you're shameless.'

'No, I'm not. Well, maybe I am. I've got my faults, God knows, and practically everything Colin said or did seemed to inflame them. It's a shame that we . . .' Her voice trailed off. She sat gazing at the curtains, her forefinger tapping abstractedly at the remnant of her cigarette.

Sally eyed her thoughtfully. 'You probably do need someone. By themselves, the children . . .'

'They're cherubs, both of them. But you can't *talk* at them as you can an adult. They live in a different world. I do get irked at times. Long to . . . stretch my intellect a bit, with a spot of ego-massage thrown in.'

'That's only natural.' Sally hesitated. 'In other circumstances, I'd say why not come back to the agency? Only we're retrenching at present, and besides . . .'

'Not a good idea, Sal, thanks all the same. I've got out

of the way of it. Looking after the house and kids is a full-time job in itself, believe me. What I really need . . .' She scowled at the table. 'What I'm really after is a nice, cosy relationship with somebody attentive but not persistent, if you know what I mean.'

Sally smiled. 'I think so. I was glancing at the *Gleaner* yesterday—the Personal column. Mother always devours it. She's fascinated by the things they say about themselves. Anyway, reading some of the ads, it struck me that this is what a large percentage of people are really seeking—an undemanding contact of some kind, nothing too heavy. Nothing possessive. Is this the kind of thing you've got in mind?'

Stubbing out the cigarette, Louise surveyed her friend quizzically, not without a touch of embarrassment. 'It's rather funny you should bring that up,' she said.

The offices of the *Gleaner* stood at a corner of the Market Square, en route to the spot where Louise had left her car. Having made sure that Sally had disappeared into the supermarket behind her, Louise walked inside and with an assumption of indifference mentioned a box number to the receptionist. After a search, she was handed a couple of envelopes, the *Gleaner's* address being typewritten on one and scrawled in green ink on the other. Thanking the poker-faced girl clearly and challengingly, she packed them into her bag and returned to the car.

She had meant to drive home first, but she couldn't wait. Turning on the radio, she slit the handwritten envelope with a sense of heart-thumping anticipation that melted like snow in August as she conned the introduction.

Albeit I am in my very early sixties, many people have been known to say that I look a great deal younger, and indeed my interests lie more in the sphere of . . .

Reading without attention to the end, she crushed the sheet and stuffed it back inside her bag before turning with diminished zest to the other. The typing was impeccable. The envelope, purple-lined, looked and felt costly. The vellum notepaper confirmed the impression. Scanning the opening line, she felt her breathing quicken.

Reaching the foot of the third and final paragraph, she pondered the signature. Maurice T. Rosenberg. Although in itself it was no more than an indecipherable wavy line, the name had been spelt out in block capitals underneath, and a telephone number had been appended. The code indicated that Maurice T. Rosenberg lived well outside the town, possibly more in the region of Abingmore. Refolding the letter, Louise inserted it carefully into a pocket of her sheepskin jacket, fired the engine, reversed competently from the parking strip and headed for home.

For the first mile, speculation about Rosenberg was uppermost in her mind. After that, by a natural progression, she started to wonder about another unknown character: the man in the car seen by Terri. Dismissively as she had treated the subject in conversation with Sally, inwardly she was perturbed. To the best of her judgement, it wasn't in Terri's nature to fabricate or imagine things. If she said she had seen a man sitting, apparently aimlessly, in a car outside the school, then he had existed. Contrary to what she had told Sally, Terri's teacher had taken the matter seriously and was putting various precautions into operation: for all this, Louise remained disquieted.

The one plus factor, if so it could be called, was that the man could scarcely be Colin himself. His reddish hair and spectacles would have been unmistakable to Terri . . . unless he had left off the glasses and worn a wig, which she supposed was feasible though hardly in character.

Anxious for a meeting with his daughter, would he have gone out of his way to make himself unrecognizable to her? Louise felt that she knew Colin pretty well. She had a catalogue of his defects permanently to hand, and top of the list was lack of imagination. A plodder. The word summarized him to perfection. If he had set out to make contact with either of the children he would, she was certain, have essayed a frontal assault, with all the built-in, fail-safe devices of an iron ball hurled from a cannon. Dark wigs? Facial adjustments? Where Colin was concerned, these things just didn't add up.

Back home, Louise did her best to put the question to the back of her mind while she poached herself an egg for lunch, then did some washing and ironing before snatching a quarter of an hour to dip into the newspapers. Two of them carried midweek holiday supplements, and Louise had bought them both. These days, she read them more from nostalgia, with a professional eye, than with any thought of taking up any of their breezy suggestions. Holidays, for the time being, were out. Colin's maintenance cheques would need to swell mightily—apart from gaining three hundred per cent in reliability—before she could even begin to consider a fortnight in the sun for herself and two minors. The best she could do, meanwhile, was to indulge in imaginary trips, like those railway fanatics who took phantom cross-country journeys over train timetables.

Surfacing from the depths of the second supplement, she glanced at the kitchen clock and saw that it was three-twenty. After two-thirty, the letter had specified. Would a fifty-minute lapse suggest an indecent eagerness? If it did, so what? She had nothing to lose. The whole thing was a bit of fun, that was all: a tiny venture into the unexplored. Let him think what he chose. Rising, she marched out to the hall and lifted the phone.

The voice that answered was female. Hardly a

promising start. Louise thought briefly about ringing off without speaking. Glancing at the letter in her free hand, she plunged.

'Is Mr Rosenberg available?'

'I maight be able to reach him. Who's calling?'

'Mrs Fletcher.'

'Can you tell me what the call is about?'

'It's a personal matter.'

'Will you hold?'

She sounded high-powered. Delay ensued. Wherever he was, Mr Rosenberg seemed to be keeping himself inaccessible: a board meeting, perhaps? Louise had expected the number to belong to a private subscriber. The fact that she had come through to what appeared to be a commercial undertaking of some magnitude was one that, after the initial shock, emboldened rather than disturbed her. She sat patiently, prepared to wait. Before long the female voice returned.

'May he call you back, Mrs Fletcher?'

'I suppose so,' Louise said haughtily. 'Will it be inside the next half-hour?'

'I would think so. If you can let me have your number . . .'

Once more in the kitchen, making a start on the children's fish pie and frozen green beans, Louise demanded of herself whether she should have told the high-powered secretary to instruct Mr Rosenberg to get lost. Had the number been a private one, she wouldn't have hesitated. But there was something reassuring about the impersonality of the set-up. It was along the lines of what she had vaguely wanted. She wondered about the name and nature of the firm. Banking? Insurance? On answering, the secretary had quoted a single name which had meant nothing to Louise . . . Baldwin's? Boulding's? Creaming the potatoes, she manufactured a shrug. After all was said and done, Mr Rosenberg was at present unimportant to her. Time enough to decide whether or not to pursue it, if and when the telephone rang.

When it did, she was watching a pan of milk coming to the boil for the custard. Forced hastily to switch off the heat, she had to leave the milk to spoil while she dashed out again to the hall. Instead of the cool control she had planned, her voice betrayed fluster. She misquoted her number. 'Ai'm sorry,' bugled the secretary. 'Ai wanted four-three-zero . . .'

'I *meant* four-three-O,' Louise corrected herself. 'Louise Fletcher speaking.'

'Mr Rosenberg on the laine for you,' the secretary said frostily, after an interval.

And a joyful Easter to you, Louise said mentally. Again she thought seriously of hanging up. Before she could transpose idea and action, a male voice came on. 'This is Mrs Louise Fletcher of the *Gleaner*?'

The enquiry, faintly ludicrous in itself, was given an arresting quality by its delivery. The voice was deep and rich, measured, self-confident. She lined up a choice of replies. None of them seemed sonorous enough to match the occasion, and finally she settled tamely for 'Louise Fletcher speaking.' Was the secretary still listening in?

Mr Rosenberg said, 'You received my letter, then, and were kind enough to call. May I apologize for having to ask you to wait? Urgent business elsewhere. Please tell me if I've called back at an inappropriate time.'

'Not at all.'

'I'm so glad. I was rather hoping we might arrange to meet. Does the idea of dinner appeal to you?'

Louise drew in a silent breath. 'That would be nice, only . . .'

'Of course,' he said instantly. 'Difficult for you. Your Press notification mentioned children. Lunch, then?'

'I could manage that. Any particular day?'

'Tomorrow?'

'How about the day after?' she countered instinctively.

'Impossible for me, I'm afraid,' he said, sounding genuinely sorrowful. 'Perhaps at some future—'

'I could possibly make it tomorrow,' she cut in, her climbdown complete and instantaneous. 'Let me just take a look at my . . . Yes, I can fit it in. What time?'

'You'd prefer to meet outside Bancester?'

'Oh no. It doesn't matter.'

'Martelli's, then, at one o'clock. Is that acceptable to you?'

'Perfectly, thank you.' By now, Louise had got the measure of the dialogue and was enjoying it rather. 'I'll see you there, Mr Rosenberg. Many thanks for calling.'

'My pleasure,' he said politely. 'I shall look forward to the occasion.' The line died.

Replacing the receiver, Louise returned slowly to the kitchen. The milk in the pan had collapsed to a scum. Rinsing it out, she poured in more from the carton and placed it back on the heater. Standing watching it, she laughed suddenly to herself.

She was still in high humour when the children arrived home. While they were eating, she said casually to Terri, 'Did you see the man today?'

'What man?' Terri was intent upon dividing her green beans into equal and manageable lengths.

'The dark-haired one in the car.'

Terri paused to reflect. 'I think so.'

'You *think*? Weren't you looking out for him?'

'Mummy, Miss Slimthorpe says we can all go to have tea with her on Friday, after school.'

Louise controlled her exasperation. 'Does that mean I've got to drive over and pick you up?'

'No,' Kevin said scornfully. 'The bus is going to take them *and* bring them back. She never gets anything right.' Brother and sister exchanged insulting faces. 'And there *was* a man,' he added, stooping to extract a comic from his school bag on the floor.

Louise felt her stomach pitch a little. 'Sitting in a car?' she asked, keeping sharpness out of her voice. 'Outside the school?'

'I don't know.' Kevin unfolded the comic. 'I mean,' he enlarged, responding to his mother's look, 'I only saw him from the back of the bus. But he was in a car, and he followed us home.'

CHAPTER 4

For a town like Bancester, Martelli's was special. It belonged to the breed of establishment where management policy seemed to be a subtle blend of cosseting and intimidation. The moment Louise set foot inside, an attendant was at hand to remove her coat and to ignore her mention of the name Rosenberg. For a dozen endless seconds she was left standing at the centre of the foyer before a second man, older, decked in black tie, slithered into her locality and breathed, 'Mr Rosenberg's guest, madam?' as though the information had been pasted to her back and he had only just spotted it. Her resolute self-control buckled a little in the heat of irritation.

'That's right. Is he here?'

'Would madam care for an apéritif?'

'I'll have a dry martini.' Almost the last thing in the world she craved at this moment was a dry martini. Such was the convention, however, and she wasn't going to deviate for the sake of this waxen replica who looked as if another hundred watts overhead would have dissolved him into the Wilton. She let him conduct her to a tiny quilted bar across a corner. The stools were blooms of scarlet upholstery on single stems of stainless steel, poised to spin at a touch, and exceedingly high. By a series of cautious gymnastics she eased herself on to one, thankful that she had opted for a mid-calf-length dress of full design. A third man appeared out of vacancy, produced a martini, set it silently before her, vanished back into the mist. She sat sipping, wishing she hadn't come.

The older man returned from wherever he had gone, rubbing his hands flakily. 'A little better,' he remarked, stationing himself between Louise and the shrouded windows, 'since this morning.'

'Pardon?'

'The weather. A faint improvement on what we've been having.'

'It could scarcely be worse. Is Mr Rosenberg here?'

'At your service.' The voice was close to her left ear.

Startled, she set her stool revolving and swept the martini off the bar with her elbow as she came round. The man at her shoulder said calmly, 'Another martini, Harold, for Mrs Fletcher, if you wouldn't mind. And the same for me. Have I kept you waiting?' A hand extended itself. 'It's good to meet visually as well as verbally. I want to thank you for keeping our appointment.'

'Thank *you*,' she stammered, at a loss.

In her mind, the image that had formed since yesterday was pear-shaped, balding and a little moist. In the flesh, Mr Maurice T. Rosenberg was none of these things. To begin with, he was younger. Not more than mid-forties, at a guess, and well preserved, stockily but trimly built, an inch or so taller than herself. Under a thatch of dark, moulded hair, a set of aquiline features was underpinned by a pair of full lips, currently parted to display an upper tier of remarkably white teeth. Eyebrows even denser than his hair gave him a statesmanlike appearance. The eyes were a light blue, perceptive though not piercing. The material of his pale grey suit bore a faint sheen. A stiff collar secured a maroon silk tie whose knot nestled at his throat like a partially-inflated toy balloon.

It was a good deal to take in, all at once. Contenting herself with a quick overall impression, Louise ransacked her brain for a more constructive donation to the exchange. 'It's not for the host to be beholden to the guest,' she said feebly, wondering whether the remark conveyed what she intended or whether it was presumptuous.

Mr Rosenberg seemed gratified. A hand slid two more martinis on to the bar counter between them: capturing one of them deftly, he raised it towards her face. 'A rare attitude, Mrs Fletcher, if I may say so. Your good health.'

Louise had the feeling that she had said something rather fortunate. Suddenly the martini tasted better. Smiling at him over the rim of the glass, she decided not to press her luck. Her reserve seemed to suit Mr Rosenberg. Eyeing her speculatively in an inoffensive way, he said after a moment, 'Are you in business, Mrs Fletcher?'

She returned his look guardedly. Had she miscalculated? There was no guile in his manner: nothing but a wish to be informed. 'I was with a travel agency, but I left when I had a family. I've since thought—'

'Always a pity,' he said, interposing without seeming to interrupt, 'when a promising career comes to a halt for reasons of that sort. Not that I'm belittling the experience of motherhood. You wouldn't have missed it, I dare say.'

'I suppose I wouldn't.'

The upper teeth showed and vanished. 'You sound a little doubtful.'

'I do?' She pretended to consider. 'Maybe I do regret not having had the chance to really . . . come to grips with a challenge. Commercially speaking, that is. It's hard to say.'

Mr Rosenberg produced a pack of expensive menthol

cigarettes and offered them. Taking one, Louise was immediately set upon by the desiccated Harold with a jet of flame which she employed to produce a surge of scented vapours. Following suit, Mr Rosenberg said meditatively, 'Domestic problems, I've always been given to understand, constitute the supreme challenge.'

'In a way, possibly.' She slipped him a glance. 'I gather you don't speak from personal experience?'

He drew deeply on his cigarette. 'It's different for men. What ages are your children, Mrs Fletcher?'

'Eight and ten.' Two could play at being terse. 'Yes, I think you're right. Men don't have the same problems.' Diluting the acid, she went on smilingly, 'But then, that's to be expected, isn't it? The motivation varies. Even between one woman and another . . .'

'I take your point.' He said it good-humouredly, but with an air of dismissing the subject. 'I won't ask about your former husband, Mrs Fletcher, as I have the feeling this may be neither the time nor the place. To be candid, ex-spouses are not especially fascinating as a topic—do you agree? Talking about them is rather like discussing last year's US Vice-President, I sometimes think.'

'Me too.' Louise uttered the falsehood without a quiver.

'I should prefer,' Mr Rosenberg continued, examining the glass between his fingers, 'to keep the conversation more up to date, if you've no objection.'

'I'm all in favour.' She gave him her brilliant, person-to-person smile, the type she had always held in reserve to call upon when asking prospective travellers whether they wanted maximum insurance or cut-price. 'Can I just make one thing clear? In my Press announcement . . .'

'Stress was laid on the word "friendship". Quite understood.'

'Also "companionship",' Louise said quickly.

'Of course. The two are the same.'

'As long as there's no confusion. I wouldn't want anyone to be . . .'

'There's no confusion, Mrs Fletcher.'

She gained the impression that he appreciated her frankness, thought better of her as a result. Abruptly she felt light-hearted, able to regard even the hovering Harold with a certain benevolence. She looked about her.

'What a pleasant meeting place this is. I'll have to add it to my list.'

He turned to examine the room before bringing his gaze back as though assessing her for height, poundage, and resistance to neon lighting. 'The surroundings seem to suit you, I must say.' Maintaining his solemn scrutiny, he gestured to Harold, who trotted across with a pair of menus. 'If we order now,' said Mr Rosenberg, handing her one, 'there'll be time for another cocktail and a further exchange of confidences before we need go through to our table. Is it my usual, Harold?'

'Certainly, Mr Rosenberg. We wouldn't put you elsewhere without your consent.'

If that's meant to impress me, Louise thought, it's succeeded. A pleasurable shiver ran down her spine.

'Don't hurry to make your choice,' her host went on, eyeing the menu with a kind of disdain. 'Harold likes his selection to be weighed carefully. Right, Harold?'

'On the nail, Mr Rosenberg.'

'So we can take our time. Unless you're under pressure, yourself?'

'Not a bit.' Taking an olive from a dish, Louise nibbled into it, beaming at him. 'I may have family commitments, but I'm quite well organized.'

Although detached, the house was narrow-fronted and looked less than substantial: the windows needed fresh paint. Having passed and re-passed it, Eva continued along to the neighbouring chalet bungalow and rang the doorbell. An elderly haggard woman put her nose out. Eva smiled at her.

'I hope I've not called at an inconvenient time. Would you by any chance be interested in Regal Products?'

'Regal . . . ?'

'I'm their new agent for the district. I'm conducting a survey to find out whether—'

'Oh no.' The nose shook itself determinedly. 'I get my stuff from the self-help. Soap powder, is it?'

'Beauty care,' Eva explained. 'Good quality, you know. But I can see you don't want to be pestered. The lady next door . . . would she be a likely customer, do you think?'

The nose developed wrinkles. 'You'd have to ask her that yourself.'

'I was hoping to. She seems to be out.'

'Try evenings.' The nose sniffed. 'She has to be in then, to see to the children. She might enjoy looking at lipsticks an' that. Sorry I can't help you further.'

'You've been very kind.' Returning to the footway, Eva walked briskly back to the other house and this time took the concrete path along to the porch. A brass knocker, puma-shaped, hung against the door. She administered a double tap with its hind paws. Almost immediately an interior door opened and there was a faintly vibrant, pattering sound, followed by a rattling. The door opened a few inches to be held by a chain. A small face peered expectantly through, and became downcast.

Eva said cheerfully, 'Hullo. Is your mother at home?'

'She's out,' the boy replied. 'She won't be back till six o'clock.'

'I'll call another time, then. I just wondered if I could interest her in some beauty aids. Regal Products. Does she use a lot of make-up?'

'She uses nail varnish,' the boy said, having considered.

'Well, we've a very good brand that might appeal to her. Will you tell her I called?'

'All right.' The door started to close.

Through the diminishing gap, Eva added, 'Have you any sisters who use make-up?'

'I've got one. She's only seven. No, eight.'

Eva laughed. 'We can rule her out, then. I expect she's having her tea?'

'She's having it with her teacher. She won't be back till six, either.'

'So you're looking after the house. Gets a bit lonesome, doesn't it?'

'No,' he said politely. 'I don't mind.'

'Perhaps you quite enjoy being on your own. Lots of peace and quiet?' He responded dutifully to her smile. 'See you again,' she added, turning to leave.

'Bye.' The door clumped into its frame.

Back inside the car, which she had left in a nearby sidestreet, Eva removed the blonde wig and shook out her own coppery hair before driving off. During the journey to Stroudbury she was deep in thought. When she arrived, there was still sufficient daylight to enable her to stow the Samba without difficulty in the crude lay-by cut into the bank outside the cottage and pick her way across the crazy paving to the kitchen door at the side. It was the only entrance to the cottage, a stone and timber relic of a past century with small ground-floor windows and minuscule upper ones that barely admitted light. Using the key that Fletcher had given her, she let herself inside, wincing at the stench of dampness that met her nostrils. Dumping the carrier of provisions she had brought with her, she switched on the electric fan heater and the transistor radio, bringing warmth and sound into the room before removing her coat and turning her attention to the cooker.

The potatoes had begun to crisp in the oven when footfalls made themselves heard on the path. She went and threw open the kitchen door, letting the light spill out. 'You're late. I thought perhaps you'd had a puncture.'

'I couldn't get away. Some daft query kept me on the phone.' Fletcher stooped to remove his bicycle clips, then straightened and stood regarding her, a shade uncertainly. He was holding a French loaf, semi-encased in a paper bag. 'How was your afternoon?'

'Interesting.' She took the loaf gently out of his hand. 'Tell you about it. Like a drink first?'

He pondered the suggestion. Wiping her fingers on a cloth, Eva moved against him. 'Tell you what,' she said softly. 'While you're recovering from the ride, why not lie down and relax for a while? The meal's under control. I'll fix us each a drink and we can—'

The sentence ended in a gasp as his arms went around her. For a while after that, the sigh of the fan heater and a faint bubbling from the cooker were the only sounds in the kitchen: Eva had flipped off the radio when hearing his approach. Presently, sensing a mounting urgency within him, she gave him an extra hug and broke clear. 'All right, love. All right. I'll switch everything off and we'll go upstairs. The electric blanket's on.'

'You think of everything.' He spoke on a gulp, watching her movements as she extinguished the oven and turned off the fan. She slipped a hand into his and he pursued her through the living-room to the precipitous, complaining staircase.

By eight-thirty they had finished eating at the kitchen table, all tension liquidated. Kept warm by the heater, the room engulfed them like an insulating jacket, locking in the glow. Music from the transistor thrummed softly. For the moment, the smell of dampness was quelled if not annihilated. Pushing her plate away, Eva leaned back and lit each of them a cigarette. The baked air became hazy.

'Snug little hideout you've got here,' she remarked.

'What century would it date from?'

Fletcher squinted around. 'Seventeenth? I'm no good on antiquity. To judge from the windows . . .'

'Airholes, you mean. The one in that bedroom of yours must have been designed to keep out squirrels. Saves on curtaining, at least.' She smiled at him through the smoke. 'Just the same, it's perfection.'

'I don't know about that. Still, I'll settle for it.'

'We could get closer.'

'How?'

She breathed vapour at the ceiling. 'You know how. Had any word from that sleuth of yours? Is he doing anything?'

'Spoke to him this morning, on the blower. He says he's building up a dossier, but it's slow work and he needs time.'

'Mm. His time, your money. I wonder if he's going to achieve anything.'

Fletcher's shoulders rose and fell. 'I'll give him a while longer. After that I may have to reconsider.'

'I'd start doing it right now, if I were you.' Eva tapped her cigarette against the edge of a plate. 'I saw Kevin this afternoon.'

Fletcher gave a jerk of the head. 'You did? Where?'

'At home.' She related what had occurred. 'If this Ferrari of yours,' she concluded, 'is meant to be keeping an eye on things, he was keeping a low profile, that's all I can say. I saw no sign of anybody.'

'He could have been watching from his car.'

'There's nowhere to wait on that main road. I had to park way round a corner.'

'If he's already picked up the information he wants . . .'

'I thought he was working full-time for you. It was just four-thirty when I got there. When does he pack up—mid-afternoon?'

'He might be chasing some other line of his own,'

Fletcher said anxiously. He thought for a moment. 'Kevin told you he wasn't expecting his mother home until six?'

'That's what he said. For all we know, it may have been later. I couldn't hang around to see.'

'Not that late, is it?'

'A ten-year-old kid, alone in the house? There should be someone waiting for him when he gets home from school.'

Fletcher nodded, said nothing.

Eva regarded him intently. 'Quite apart from which, Terri was also due back at six, and if Louise still wasn't there . . .'

'We're surmising, rather.'

'Of course we are. And yet you're paying for concrete information that you're not getting.'

'He's compiling this dossier,' Fletcher reminded her. 'There was no agreement that he should keep me briefed from day to day.'

'Well, I think there should have been.' She touched his arm. 'Sorry, love. I'm only interfering because . . . I just get so uptight about it, on your behalf.'

'I know.' He put a hand on hers.

'To my mind, she calmly gets away with whatever she chooses and there seems not a thing you can do about it.'

'There is. If I can get evidence of neglect.'

An impatient sound escaped from Eva. 'If you did, it would need to be pretty harrowing to convince a court that she's not a fit person to have charge of them. I know what my brother Jock went through. His wife was an absolute slut with no sense of right or wrong, she lived the life of an alley-cat but she still managed to keep hold of their daughter for four years until finally one of her boyfriends . . . I won't say what happened, but it did actually persuade a judge that a new arrangement might possibly be called for, and my brother got Hilary back. By that time she was an emotional mess. You want that to happen to Terri?'

'You know I don't. In Louise's case, I can't imagine . . . But at present she's having it all her own way, I agree, and this is what I'm trying to fight.'

'Then *fight* it.'

'I'm doing all I can.'

'You're doling out cash, day by day, but are you likely to get a proper return? You've no hold on this gumshoe. What's to prevent him spinning out his "investigations" to kingdom come, at your expense?'

'I told you, I shan't let it drag on. Besides, if he doesn't deliver, he loses his two hundred quid bonus.'

'If he makes enough in the meantime, that won't break his heart. Look, I tell you what.' Bringing her other arm across, Eva rested it on Fletcher's shoulder and looked him steadily in the eyes. 'Give him another week. Then ask to see the dossier, and if it's a dud—or, which is more to the point, if it doesn't exist—then give Ferrari the boot and we'll tackle it my way. Fair enough?'

Fletcher blinked. 'I'm making no promises. Your way sounds chancy.'

'It could produce quick results.'

'We'd be foul of the law afterwards. Child-snatching fathers don't exactly commend themselves to the courts.'

'Who cares? The law does nothing for you: just keeps stringing you along. Which counts more? Legal niceties, or our future with the children? We have to decide.'

'It would mean going abroad, starting an entirely new life . . .'

'Anything wrong with that?' she asked teasingly, leaning forward to kiss the tip of his nose.

'Okay,' he said after a pause. 'Let's give it a week. Then we'll see.'

She kissed him again, on the mouth with a scent of lamb-fat. 'To get what you want in this life, you have to go out and grab it. There's no other way.'

CHAPTER 5

'Champagne?' Sally was impressed. 'My! Some lunch.'

'My dear, that was nothing.' Slicing her scone, Louise eyed her friend with the complacency of one who has stores to bestow upon a deserving case. 'The meal was fantastic—take out a mortgage and try Martelli's yourself some time—but all he said was, he'd like to take me somewhere *special* next time. Oh, I realize he was showing off. But I ask you.'

'How did you react?' Sally demanded. 'Did you pretend you'd seen better?'

'Just kept my cool . . . I think. Tried not to seem over-impressed. I've an idea that's what he wanted.'

'He's after someone sophisticated?'

'He certainly doesn't seem to be aiming down-market. And I may be wrong, but he didn't strike me as a womanizer. One can't always tell, I know. I could be in for a horrible shock. So far, all he seems interested in is finding out whether I can sit with him in the right surroundings without dropping my aitches.'

'And you? What's your opinion of *him*?'

Louise paused in her buttering of the scone. 'I'm not one to draw spot conclusions, I hope. He took me for a drive afterwards—Mercedes, uniformed chauffeur, the works—and I did learn a little about him, though not much. He's in property. Commercial premises, I fancy. He operates nationwide, and he's a widower. That's it. Like a lot of his type, he tells you as much as he wants you to know, then clams up.' Picking out a sultana, she chewed it reflectively. 'One thing, though, does stick out a mile. He's not pushed for a penny.'

'In that case, why . . .' Sally hesitated.

'Why is he answering a newspaper ad for a female companion? He did explain that. He wants somebody who's completely unconnected with his work. The only people he normally rubs shoulders with, you see, are business contacts. What he's after is a matey relationship with an outsider. Someone passable-looking, with enough social poise not to disgrace him when he takes her to the various functions he has to attend.'

'Such as yourself?'

'Well, after all, I'm available.'

Sally meditated. 'Since he's got all this money, I still don't see why he couldn't just hire somebody from an escort agency.'

'Too impersonal. If he's taking somebody around, he wants it to be a person he can get to know. I can understand that. I told him so.'

A chuckle came from Sally. 'I'll bet. Well, Louise love—best of luck, and here's to a fruitful association. How will you manage about the children?'

Louise looked at her blankly. 'Manage?'

'I mean, if he wants you to go places at odd times. Could be awkward, couldn't it?'

'They're very capable. They both lunch at school, and if it's an early evening affair I can leave their meals on the warmer. The only problem might be a late function, but I'll cross that bridge when I come to it.'

'If it weren't for Mother, I could come round and babysit.'

'My dear, there's no need. I'm used to coping. Being an only child and an orphan, I've had to. We'll be fine. Actually, we've already had a trial run.'

Sally examined her across the table. 'Trial run?'

'Rosenberg asked me out again—Friday afternoon. He wanted to buy me a couple of long dresses. It was a good opportunity, because Terri was going to be late home after having tea with her teacher. So I went.'

'Wow. Get anything?'

'I'll say. We went to Rosalind's at Cheltenham. I dug out the most perfect little black-and-silver number, and then the girl found one in royal blue satin that just wanted taking in a little at the waist, so we're having that done and I should get the pair of them at the end of the week, special delivery. I daren't tell you what they cost.'

'I won't ask. Rosenberg coughed up without a murmur?'

'No.' Louise smiled mischievously. 'He didn't think they were good enough. I had quite a job convincing him. Can you imagine? If that had been Colin, he'd have been crawling for the exit with his credit card strapped to his stomach. No, correction. We'd never have been inside the shop in the first place.'

'Most husbands would feel the same,' Sally observed chidingly. 'You were in a unique position, let's face it. Did he buy you anything else, while he was at it?'

'Just tea, on the way home. A super little place on the bank of a river in a village called . . . I forget. I only know it was perfect. The one thing wrong with the afternoon was his chauffeur.'

'Couldn't he drive?'

'Oh, I couldn't fault his driving. It's just that he was kind of a wet blanket. Damp, anyhow. Thin and sandy-haired and a bit gaunt, with a dour manner. I got the feeling he disapproved of me.'

'You can't have everything. What's his name?'

'Jackson.'

'It would be, wouldn't it? What time did you get home?'

'Some time after six,' Louise said vaguely. 'I hardly noticed—I was so buzz-headed with the afternoon. Big greeting from the pair, needless to say.'

'You're not bothered about them being alone in the house?'

'It was just for an hour or two,' Louise protested. 'Kevin always keeps the doors locked and on the chain. In an emergency, he'd dial 999. As a last resort, he could sprint next door and rouse old Mrs Willerby, though what use she'd be I can't conceive. She's always practically ignored us.'

'Suppose someone called at the door? Looking innocent, but—'

'What an old fusspot you are, Sal. Kevin would never let anyone inside. Someone did call on Friday, as a matter of fact.'

'Oh? Who?'

'Some woman, trying to flog cosmetics. Regal Products. Ever heard of them? Me neither. Well, that's the bulletin up to date. How about your end?'

'Just the usual.' Picking up her gloves, Sally reached automatically for the bill. 'Package trips by day, keeping Mother amused by night. I wonder,' she added thoughtfully, tugging on the left-hand glove, 'whether I should place an ad in the *Gleaner*? They seem to get results.'

Soon after one o'clock, the telephone rang. Licking duck pâté off her fingers, Louise answered the call and spoke to Mr Rosenberg's dynamic secretary.

'This afternoon?' she said, having listened. 'I don't know . . . It might be difficult. What time?'

'Mr Rosenberg would laike you to be available at three.'

Why did she feel no resentment? The summons verged on the peremptory. 'About what time,' she found herself asking, 'would I be home?'

'Quaite by seven. Mr Rosenberg would laike you to be assured of that.'

Louise thought swiftly. Episode four of the Dickens TV serial was on early this evening: that would keep the children spellbound until six-thirty. And she could probably contrive a slightly earlier homecoming, anyway. 'That'll be all right, tell Mr Rosenberg. Short cocktail dress?'

'Quaite suitable. The car will be along sharp at three. Thank you, Mrs Fletcher. Good afternoon.'

Clearing away the remnants of her lunch, Louise played a mental spotlight over her wardrobe. The navy-blue dress with crimson trimmings? She suspected it might appeal to Mr Rosenberg. Also she felt comfortable in it: a plus factor. It would go nicely with her new shoes and the evening bag, hardly used, that Sally had given her last Christmas. On the other hand, the green satin dress with panels might be safer. No sense in living too dangerously, first time out.

Preoccupied by the dilemma, she grilled a pair of cod fillets, added chips and peas, put the plates on the warmer, planted half a cottage loaf and some butter on the kitchen table, and against the butter dish leaned a note in block capitals: EAT THE LOT! HAD TO GO OUT UNEXPECTEDLY. WON'T BE LONG. LOVE, MUM. Then she darted upstairs and opened her wardrobe doors.

When the Mercedes arrived, punctually at three, she was faintly relieved to see from her bedroom window that it was not being driven by the dour Jackson. In his place was a taller, stringier individual with receding brown hair festooned about his ears and—as she discovered upon descending—a taciturn manner which nevertheless was easier to take than Jackson's air of suppressed condemnation. Introducing himself as Scott, he explained that Jackson had fallen sick. Hypocritically, Louise asked him to pass the invalid her condolences and stepped regally into the back of the car, glad that she had opted for the crimson-trimmed dress which went nicely beneath the short, simulated-fur jacket that had been Colin's last voluntary gesture in her direction: she had chosen, he had paid. Notwithstanding the source of its acquisition, she had always liked it as a garment. On a day such as this, cold but dry, it served admirably.

Having closed the car door upon her, Scott returned to the driver's seat and eased the street away behind them. She waited for him to U-turn at the roundabout.

Instead of doubling back, he steered through it and straight on, heading east. After a mile or so, she said, 'I thought the reception was at Gloucester. Aren't we going straight there?'

'No, ma'am. I've instructions to call at Upper Barling first. Mr Rosenberg will join us there.'

He certainly got around, she thought, settling back into the upholstery. What business deal could be engaging him at a place called Upper Barling? It was no concern of hers, but everything about Mr Rosenberg fired her curiosity. She longed to know more about him and his activities: at the same time, his inscrutability in itself was exciting. Louise liked a dash of mystery.

To an extent, this had been the trouble with Colin. He was basically, transparently, boringly honest. One always knew precisely where one stood with him, and where was the fun in that? Most people needed spice in their lives. Like Mercedes cars, chauffeurs called Jackson and Scott, journeys in the direction opposite to that which one had been expecting. They were now travelling with a brisk smoothness along a secondary road between stretches of conifer forest, a region unfamiliar to her. As they crossed an intersection, she spotted a sign which displayed place-names she had never heard of . . . Little Dean, Woodbury, East Catlow. There was no mention of Upper Barling. After another mile, she leaned forward.

'How far is it to this place?'

'Far enough.'

Scott's gaze remained fixed ahead. The slight oddness of the reply was no encouragement to dig further:

nevertheless she persevered. 'Will it take us long to get from there to Gloucester? It's my children, you see. I mustn't be too—'

'I wouldn't worry yourself about them, Mrs Fletcher.'

'It's not that I'm worrying. I only want to—'

'Just relax. Mr Rosenberg wants you to take things easy. They were his instructions. He'd like you to enjoy the ride.'

Louise felt her lips compress. She waited a moment before replying. 'That's kind of Mr Rosenberg. He knows my situation, of course. I'm sure he'd have no intention . . .'

Once more she lost the end of a sentence as they took a corner. A signpost at the far side of the junction had caught her eyes. After brief hesitation she said, 'Upper Barling was to the right, I thought. The arrow pointed that way.'

'Town lies over there.' Scott adapted the car's pace to the lane, which was barely more than single-track. 'We're not going to the town.'

Frustrated, Louise sat back. There seemed little to be gained from quizzing this robotic wheel-spinner; better to wait until Mr Rosenberg joined the party. Against his driver, he would show up as positively garrulous. Composing herself, she did her best to appreciate the landscape, now unquestionably in the category of English Rural, Parkland Division, Grade One. The sky had cleared to allow the plunging sun to distribute rays almost horizontally over the countryside, giving it a luminous and yet faintly disquieting quality, like that of a beautiful living-room invaded by a burglar's torch. Seen in passing, the view was fine. Louise found that she had lost interest. It was like being driven through a valuable oil-painting that didn't really suit its place on the wall. She made a move to lean forward again, changed her mind, resettled herself uneasily. How many miles, she wondered, had they covered already? Consulting her watch, she found that it had turned four o'clock.

Her sense of direction lay in tatters. Dimly, she had a notion that they had been heading consistently away from Gloucester: if so, the city must lie many miles to the west, a distance at least equivalent to that which they had covered.

She could be wrong. Where was the sun? Scott had the radiance of it full on the back of his neck. She was right. They were still driving due east. This was getting ridiculous.

'Look, I don't want to make a silly fuss, but I—'

'Don't, then.'

The sheer crudity of the retort made her catch her breath. For a few simmering moments she sat in silence, trying to fix upon a line. Was it worth a scene? Either she ignored the incident or she blasted the man out of his seat: there was no middle way. If she compounded the unpleasantness, Mr Rosenberg might be put out. It could be that he was used to the verbal vagaries of Scott, accepted them, would think less of her if she took outraged exception.

On the other hand, he might think her a wet fish if she didn't. Coupled with her own feelings, this consideration decided her. She tapped Scott heftily on the left shoulder.

'One more remark like that, laddie, and you and I will be on collision course. Clear?'

He drove on in silence. Satisfied that she had made her point, Louise waited half a mile before saying on a more conciliatory note, 'Much further? If it is, say so and we'll turn round here, if you don't mind. Time's running out. I'll square things with Mr Rosenberg later.'

Wordlessly, Scott braked and swung the car into a nearside gateway. This was it, then. A pity, but she'd been right to take a firm line. Even Scott had come to realize the senselessness of the detour. Bracing herself against the expected halt, she watched in rigid astonishment as the yellowstone gate pillars slid past on either flank and the car surged on down an asphalted track between fallow fields towards a white-painted, five-barred gate at the foot of the incline. For a moment she thought Scott was going to smash straight through it. Braking viciously, so that this time she was flung forward, he brought the car to a bouncing stop at the edge of the cattle-grid guarding the gate, opened the car door, jumped out and slammed it again.

Nursing a bruised forearm, Louise observed him open-mouthed as he released the gate-catch and swung it back, securing it with a bolt shot into a pipe protruding from the ground.

She wrenched at the door-handle to her right.

It wouldn't move. She tried the nearside one, with the same result. Scott was tramping back, eyeing her expressionlessly through the glass. As he unlocked and pulled open the driver's door she was starting to clamber between the front seat neck-restraints; placing the palm of a hand against her chin, he impelled her back with a kind of slow-motion violence, returning her unceremoniously to the rear cushions. Slamming the door, he drove forward.

Louise gathered breath to scream.

CHAPTER 6

'It was my idea,' said Eva, changing gear at the T-junction, 'so I don't mind taking the initiative. If she gets uppity, I won't push it.'

'Promise?' Fletcher demanded worriedly.

'Love, of course I do. Trust me.'

'Only Louise can be . . . unpredictable. If she felt she was being hounded, she'd be perfectly capable of moving out, lock stock and barrel, and disappearing with them. Then we'd be worse off than ever.'

'I don't know so much.' Emerging from the one-way system in the heart of Bancester, Eva accelerated back into top gear before resuming. 'If she did that, it would put her in the wrong—there's still an access order in force, don't forget. With a couple of kids, she'd find it tricky to vanish entirely. Sooner or later they'd be traced. Then you might stand a chance at least of getting the order enforced. But in any case, I don't believe Louise would take such a drastic step. She's sitting comfortably here, nice house, money coming in. Why risk all that?'

'If she felt pressurized . . .'

Removing her left hand from the wheel, Eva dealt him an affectionate jab. 'Did anyone ever tell you? You see shadows when they aren't there. Don't you see, love? *You're* the one under pressure. What she's trying to do is force you to relinquish any rights over the children—shove you out of their lives. You're not going to sit down meekly under that?'

'I've already said,' he replied, low-voiced. 'I'll fight any way I can.'

Light flooded from several windows at the front of the house, as though someone were going from room to room in search of something. 'Doesn't exactly economize, does she?' Eva remarked, nosing the car into the driveway and switching off. 'But then, why should she? On somebody else's money?'

They sat in silence, surveying the illuminations. A curtain of the main downstairs window was jerked to one side, then released. Eva unhitched her seat-belt. 'You think she has look-outs posted? It would never surprise me. The way she . . .'

The front door opened and a small form emerged into the porch. Swapping glances, they left the car and went towards it. Fletcher crouched, held out both arms.

'Hi, Terri. I've called to see you. Were you expecting me?'

After some hesitation she advanced within reach. 'I thought you were my mummy,' she announced, allowing herself to be kissed on a cheek.

Fletcher looked up. Kevin had appeared in the doorway. 'Isn't she here?'

'She hasn't come home.' Terri gave a brief sniff.

Kevin said on a note of tremulous detachment, 'I keep telling her, Mum won't be long. She left a note.'

Lifting Terri, who placed a hand tentatively on his neck, Fletcher gestured to Eva and they made their way into the house. Kevin regarded them with a mixture of relief and wariness. 'This is my friend, Eva,' Fletcher told them both. 'She wanted to be introduced to you, so we thought we'd pop along.'

He glanced at the antique grandfather clock in a corner of the hall. The hands stood at six minutes to eight. 'What time,' he asked casually, 'did your mother go out?' Planting Terri on the hall chair, he kept a supportive arm about her.

'Don't know.' The quiver in Kevin's voice was closer to the surface. 'She wasn't here when we got home from school.'

Eva looked inquiringly at Fletcher. 'Around four?'

'It would be, yes.' He was keeping his own voice light and level, masking the indignation that seethed beneath. 'I should say Mum's broken down somewhere, wouldn't you? On a country road, maybe, where she can't get to a phone.'

'She didn't take the car,' Kevin volunteered. 'It's in the garage. I looked.'

'Then she's missed a bus or train. She'll be home shortly. Meanwhile, don't you think we ought to douse a few of these lights? Her electricity bill is going to be horrendous.'

'Terri put them on. She didn't like the house being all dark.'

'I think,' Eva said quickly, 'that was a very sensible thing to do. Dark houses don't appeal to me, either. Had anything to eat?'

'Mum left us some fish. I didn't finish mine.'

'Terri, did you eat yours?'

'She kept on getting up to go to the window,' Kevin said with brotherly derision. 'It got cold.'

Eva made decisively for the kitchen, the door to which stood wide open. 'You must both be starving. I'll fix you something.'

Fletcher watched her go. Under his pose of calmness, fury and disbelief smouldered like the fuse of a rocket, nudging him to the very brink of blast-off. What restrained him was the feel of Terri pressed lightly against him: he had almost given up hope of experiencing that again. He wished Kevin would move closer, make contact. The boy was gazing resolutely the other way: he gave the impression that he would have returned to the kitchen if Eva had not been in occupation, rattling dishes and cutlery as though she had been preparing meals there for years. Presently, with a small involuntary shrug, he opened the door to the rear living-room and went through. 'It's quite warm in here,' he said across a shoulder. 'I turned the heating on.'

'Good lad,' said Fletcher. 'Did you watch *David Copperfield?* There's a comedy show at eight. You two settle down and have a laugh while Eva and I whack up some supper.'

Swinging Terri to the floor, he gave her a pat which sent her trotting obediently in the wake of her brother. Shutting the door behind them, Fletcher joined Eva in the kitchen. 'What do you think?' he asked.

She finished cracking eggs into a teacup before replying. 'What do I think? For starters, I think that sleuth of yours ought to be shot. Is he supposed to have been keeping tabs on them, or isn't he?'

'Not in a protective way,' Fletcher said in half-hearted defence.

'Don't dredge up excuses for him. It makes me sick. I don't believe he's been doing a thing for his money. If he had, I'll bet he could have handed you evidence by the bundle, long before now.'

'This could be the first time she's—'

'On the very evening we happen to call? Some coincidence. Besides, I know for a fact she's done it before. When I called here, Friday afternoon, Kevin told me he wasn't expecting her home until six—and we don't know how unpunctual she was that time, either. I've a good mind to ask him.'

'Let's get some food into them first. I wonder if Kevin remembers you as the Regal Products lady.'

'No. I wore a wig and disguised my voice. Far as they're concerned, I'm just a friend of yours.'

'Where can Louise have got to, Eva? I can't believe she'd wilfully stay out like this. She has her faults, God knows, but she's not a monster.'

'On that,' Eva said sceptically, whisking the eggs, 'I'm prepared to reserve judgement.'

Bidding the children good night through their bedroom doors, Fletcher returned downstairs. 'Five past ten,' he said agitatedly, rejoining Eva in the living-room. 'Something *must* have happened. I'm going to call the police.'

When he came back, Eva looked up from a copy of *Country Life*. 'How did they react?'

'They didn't seem too bothered.' Fletcher slumped into a chair. 'Said she'd probably show up before midnight, but if she's not back by morning I'm to contact them again. They've not heard of any road or rail accidents in the area.' He scratched his scalp. 'Beats me, Eva. Say what you like about Louise, the idea of her simply roaming off for the night, leaving the kids to—'

'It doesn't beat me,' Eva said bluntly. 'From what you've told me, it seems pretty much in character.'

'Maybe I've given the wrong impression.'

'Colin, love, you have to face it. Some women are like that. You read about them all the time. They're irresponsible. I can almost read Louise's thoughts. Oh, Kevin's a big chap now, he can cope. Why shouldn't I have a good time? There's nothing . . .'

Fletcher's head was shaking. 'I'd never have said she was that mad about a "good time". Home comforts, yes. Financial security. And she's fairly easily bored, so she might feel the urge to go places now and then . . . but out up to ten-thirty at night, without letting the children know where she was?'

'She did leave them a note.'

'*Won't be long*. That's all. If she'd gone to the cinema, alone or with someone, wouldn't she have said so—and specified the time she'd be back?'

'What you're now saying about her,' Eva said, after a pause, 'seems a bit at odds with your previous comments. You're paying a man to dig up evidence of neglect. If you don't think she's capable of neglect, what's the point?'

'I'm not saying she . . .' Fletcher gestured tiredly. 'It's hard to put into words. You know my current opinion of Louise. But she's still mother of my children and I can't bring myself to accept that she'd willingly do this to them.'

Casting aside the magazine, Eva rose and came over to him. 'Love,' she said gently, encircling his neck with an arm, 'don't let your own civilized feelings block the view. All right—perhaps Louise has been unavoidably delayed tonight. The fact remains, she's left a couple of infants alone and scared in a house, in the dark, and apparently made no attempt to alert anyone about them. Okay: let's chalk it up against her. Let's make sure the authorities get to hear about it. In the long run, it could help you to regain custody and solve all our problems. You must see that.'

Fletcher nodded sombrely. 'You're right, of course. It's what I've—we've been aiming for. I just find it . . .'

'You can't think that badly of people. I know.' She kissed the top of his head.

'Is that Terri?' he asked suddenly. 'Calling out?'

While he was upstairs, investigating, Eva made coffee and familiarized herself a little more with the kitchen. On Fletcher's return she said, 'Was she having a nightmare?'

'Probably. She was on the landing, wanting to know if her mother was home.' Accepting a cup of coffee, he stood with his back to the cooker, staring into space. Partly to himself, he added, 'I could throttle Louise for this.'

'The woman next door—Mrs Willerby. Any use finding out if she knows anything?'

Fletcher's attention drifted back. 'She takes very little interest. But I suppose there'd be no harm in asking.'

He went out to the street and surveyed the chalet bungalow. Light showed in the hall, so he approached the front door and pressed the bellpush. After a lengthy delay, feet shuffled to the other side of the glazed panel. A voice quavered, 'Who is it? What do you want?'

'Mrs Willerby? It's Colin Fletcher, from next door. Can you spare a moment? I'd like to inquire about Mrs Fletcher.'

In the course of an interval, she seemed to be thinking it over. Finally, as the climax to a metallic tattoo, the door creaked inwards and her face appeared around the edge, appraising him gingerly. 'What about Mrs Fletcher?'

'I wondered if you'd seen her, at all. She hasn't come

home, you see. She didn't chance to tell you where she was going?'

'Tell *me*?' Mrs Willerby sounded cynical.

'I realize you're not in the habit of communicating much. It's just that—'

'I did see her take off.'

'Ah. What time was that?'

Mrs Willerby sucked in the vestiges of her right cheek. 'Three o'clock? Yes, it was just about an hour before the school bus stopped outside. I always hear that.'

'She left on foot?'

'No. Swanned off in style, she did. A car called for her.'

'What kind of a car?' The sharpness of his query brought a flinch out of her: he did his best to atone. 'Can you recall? It might be important.'

A big one, was all Mrs Willerby could say. Dark-coloured, certainly. 'But as to the make, I couldn't tell you, not if you was to write me out a cheque. Never did interest me, cars. I did wonder for a minute . . .'

'Yes, Mrs Willerby?'

'I did think it might be a police car.'

'Why's that?'

'The driver wore a peaked cap. I don't reckon he was, though. Police, I mean. The rest of his uniform wasn't right.'

'Chauffeur-driven vehicle . . .' Fletcher speculated. 'I don't suppose you happened to spot what Mrs Fletcher was wearing?'

Mrs Willerby believed she had been looking quite smart. 'But then, I wasn't taking that much heed. I was just straightening the curtains at the upstairs window, and I was just glancing out when she—'

'Yes, of course, I understand.' Fletcher apologized for troubling her. 'We're—I'm getting a little anxious, that's all. If I hadn't called this evening, the children would have been on their own all this time.'

'Dear me.' Mrs Willerby looked vaguely shocked.

'As it was,' he added, driving the point home, 'they were getting a bit frantic when I arrived. I can't understand what's keeping their mother away so long.'

Mrs Willerby blinked up at him guilelessly. 'Always been one for getting about, hasn't she? Likes her freedom.'

'Learn anything?' asked Eva, on his return.

He gave her a summary. 'Sounds as if she was off to a function of some kind. Quite a grand affair, possibly—but what and where? We're none the wiser.'

'Mrs Willerby is, though,' Eva pointed out.

'How do you mean?'

'She should be able to provide some useful corroborative evidence, in due course.'

Fletcher nodded abstractedly. 'I'm trying to think,' he muttered. 'Louise has a bosom friend called Sally, or had . . . but what's her surname? She might know something.'

'Is there a book of phone numbers?'

A drawer of the telephone stand yielded the leather-bound index that Fletcher had purchased for common use at the start of married life. The sole entry under 'S' was someone called Solomon, which after some effort he recalled as the surname of a couple with whom Louise had once or twice swapped babysitting duties in the early days. He went through the pages. Under 'W' he found the name Sally Wentworth, with an address and number. He gave his wristwatch a glance. Eleven-twenty. He dialled ruthlessly.

Absorbed by the exploits of Fiona Drake, ward sister at St Jude's, Sally became aware in stages of the telephone's summons. By the time it had filtered through to the top level, she knew that the caller must be on the point of giving up. Hoisting herself out of bed, she hauled on a wrap and hurried through to the central hallway. At this hour, it had to be a wrong number. She lifted the receiver. 'Yes?'

The voice was unknown to her. 'Pardon me, but is that Miss Wentworth? It's Colin Fletcher speaking. I believe my ex-wife—'

'Oh! Yes!' Collecting herself, Sally dropped her voice by an octave. 'I'm a friend of Louise, that's quite right. She's told me . . .' She caught herself on the rim. 'We never met, did we?' she substituted carefully.

'I don't think so. Look, I'm terribly sorry to disturb you . . .'

'Quite all right. Is it about Louise? Not in trouble, is she?'

'We're not sure. I was rather hoping she might be with you.'

'With *me?* Should she be?'

'I've no idea. It's merely that she went out this afternoon and hasn't arrived back. I thought possibly—'

'That's not like Louise. I don't like the sound of it.' Sally chewed her lip. 'What about the children?'

'I and a friend of mine are with them at the moment. I hardly know what to think. The police have no report of any accident and of course she may turn up before long, but one can't help feeling puzzled. You wouldn't happen to know whether she'd something special on today?'

Sally gazed at the opposite wall. She said slowly, 'I did see Louise this morning. She mentioned nothing specific then.'

'Gave no hint of anything?'

'She did refer to a . . . person. Someone she'd met.'

'Mind if I ask who?' Fletcher's voice sounded more alert.

'I'm afraid I don't know him,' Sally replied truthfully.

There was a brief pause. 'Did she say anything about meeting him this evening?'

'No. I got the impression they weren't due to see each other again until the end of the week.'

'Where?'

'Pardon?'

'I'm sorry. I meant, do you have any idea where this . . . friend of hers lives?'

'Strictly speaking, I'm not sure he'd rank as a *friend*. She's only just made his acquaintance. His background,' added Sally, again with perfect truth, 'is a total mystery to me. Apart from his name, Louise told me very little. I don't think she knew a lot herself.'

When Fletcher spoke again, he sounded apologetic and yet challenging. 'You wouldn't feel disposed to give me the name?'

Sally hesitated. 'The children were left on their own, you say?'

'Completely. If my friend and I hadn't dropped by . . .'

'The name,' she told him with some reluctance, 'is Rosenberg. More than that I can't say, I'm afraid, except that I gather he deals in property.'

'Would you know if he runs a large, chauffeur-driven car?'

'Yes, Louise did mention that. A Mercedes, I think she said.'

'Well . . . thank you, Miss Wentworth. You've been most kind and I'm sorry to have troubled you.'

'I'd sooner you called me Sally. Louise and I have known each other a long time. Look, if there's anything I can do, any practical help needed . . .'

'We've got everything in hand. Thanks again. Good night.'

He rang off, leaving Sally with her mouth ajar. Replacing the receiver, she kept her hand upon it while pondering matters. A cold draught nipped at her neck, prompting her to raise the collar of the wrap and head back for her bedroom door. As she did so, a voice drifted thinly from the second bedroom. With a faint sigh, she altered course.

'It's all right, Mother. Just Louise's ex-husband. He thought she might be here.'

'He must know we've only the two bedrooms.' Elderly Mrs Wentworth looked like a museum piece, propped up in bed with her teeth missing, a stole half-camouflaging her bony shoulders.

'Not staying the night, necessarily. In actual fact,' said Sally, punching up her mother's pillows, 'he knows next to nothing about us. I've never even met him.'

'How does he sound?'

'Anxious. With reason, I'd say. It sounds very much as though Louise has gone off and abandoned the children.'

'That's not very nice. I thought you said she was a decent sort?'

'She is. I can't understand it.' Frowning fixedly at the bed-head, Sally lost herself in reflections. 'It makes no sense,' she murmured, emerging to give her mother a peck on the forehead and switch off the bedside lamp. She stood for a moment in the darkness, thinking hard. 'Louise just isn't that kind of person,' she added presently, more to herself than her parent. 'I do hope she's all right.'

CHAPTER 7

First into the office, Fletcher smacked open the top window to dispel the fug, shut it again to seal out the wind, sat at his desk, picked up the phone. He dialled.

Waiting, he eyed with intense distaste the documents cluttering his in-tray. The line clicked. He said tentatively, 'Hullo?' Answered by silence, he went on, 'I'd like to place an order. A food hamper for two at midday, please.' He hung up.

‘ ’Morning, Mr Fletcher.’ Irene, the smaller and prettier of the two juniors, greeted him with her customary blithe disregard as she arrived in a whirl of garments which she proceeded to distribute about the room as a prelude to extended auto-analysis before the mirror by the door. ‘Early today, aren’t we?’ She moulded a blonde tress into revised geometry beneath her left earlobe. ‘Have trouble sleeping?’

‘Breakfast TV drove me out of the house,’ he prevaricated. ‘Irene, I shall be going off to lunch at twelve, and I may be a bit late back. Mrs Maynard won’t be in at all today. Can you and Polly stagger your lunch breaks?’

‘Okay. Mrs Maynard not well? She seemed fine yesterday.’

‘She has some domestic commitments.’

After dictating five letters of reassurance to apprehensive sellers, Fletcher felt the onset of an ache behind the eyes which no amount of finger-pressure or neck-massage seemed able to relieve. When Polly brought coffee, he swallowed an aspirin with it before making another call. There was a delay before Eva answered.

‘Thought you might have gone shopping,’ he said. ‘Any problems?’

‘All under control.’ Her calm voice was in itself an analgesic. ‘They’ve both trotted off to school. I told them their mum had been called away unexpectedly, and I’d be looking after them for a day or so.’

‘Did they swallow it?’

‘They both seem to be wearing it for the moment.’

‘Anyone been in touch?’

‘A policeman called. Sergeant Dawson. Said he spoke to you when—’

‘That’s right. I called in at the station on my way here. Seems an obliging type.’

‘Civilized. He asked a few questions, took a look

around. Murmured something about contacting the social services. I think I managed to convince him there was no need, for the present. If Louise doesn't show up by tonight, he'll want to see you again.'

Fletcher composed six more letters, divided them between the girls, told them there was no hurry and left the building. Walking briskly along to the main entrance of the supermarket, he waited the four minutes to noon before taking a trolley and wheeling it inside. The air-conditioning jolted temporary clarity back into his head. Loitering at the meat section, he picked out a sirloin of beef, examined it, squinted at the price, dropped it back, selected another. From there he moved along to the frozen chickens.

While he was choosing between a five-pounder and a bag of pieces, an arthritic hand reached past him to lift a glaciated duckling clear of its nest. Ferrari's voice said in his ear, 'If you want to ask questions—shoot. I'm listening.'

In an irritable undertone Fletcher said, 'The first question is, do we have to adopt this farcical procedure? You'd think we were discussing affairs of State.'

'Much handier for me,' averred Ferrari, wounded. 'Saves wasting valuable time in coffee bars. Also more discreet.' Encased in turtle-neck sweater and baggy windcheater, he employed his handicapped fingers to rotate the duckling in critical fashion before lowering it carefully to the base of his own trolley. 'Don't tell me. Progress report?'

'My ex-wife,' said Fletcher, reaching for a packet of stuffing, 'has now disappeared. Were you by any chance aware of that?'

The investigator stared down at a display of trussed geese, laid out like a pile of over-inflated rugby footballs coated with cream gloss paint. 'Since when?'

'Since yesterday afternoon. Of course, you could hardly

be expected to know. You're only on eight quid a day plus expenses, tax-free.'

'Barely a living wage,' Ferrari observed, fingering the plump breast of a goose.

'You seem able to afford a delicacy or two.'

'If you were my one iron in the fire, Mr Fletcher, I'd starve.'

'Now we're getting closer.' Turning, Fletcher leaned against the rim of the freezer and subjected the other to a hostile scrutiny. 'I'm sharing you, is that it? The case isn't getting your undivided attention, even though—'

'I've given it as much time as the payment merits. Be reasonable.'

'What have you accomplished? Tell me.'

'It's all on paper.'

'Show me.'

'Do you carry your files around?'

'Give me a verbal summary. What details of significance have you dug out regarding my ex's daily movements? That's a simple enough request.'

With a nudge of an elbow, Ferrari moved him along to the hams and tongues. 'Same as most people's—tend to follow a pattern. Shopping a.m., coffee with female friend, back home to . . .'

'Did I ask for trivia of that sort?' Fletcher hissed. "Offbeat excursions—they're what I was interested in. Evenings in particular. What about them?'

'Had you been paying me overtime . . .'

'I've paid you to get results. How you went about it was up to you. If you wanted more for evening work, you should have said so.'

'I did work a few evenings.' Ferrari weighed a Suffolk ham.

'Terrific. Congratulations. Spot anything?'

'Since you mention it, not a lot. She—'

'Your luck seems to have been putrid. I and a friend

have found out more, simply by calling at the house on the offchance a couple of times. For your information, my ex was late home on at least one occasion last week. Now she's faded out altogether. When were you proposing to tell me that?'

'I was planning to case the house tonight. I'd have—'

'Just what have I been paying you for, Ferrari? Can you tell me?'

Setting his trolley in motion, the investigator steered with dignity for the tinned beans. He began lifting them down, tin after tin, as Fletcher caught up with him, used his own appliance to hem him against the shelving. 'You're off the job,' he proclaimed, 'as from today. And I want a rebate of half the cash you've had from me in the past two weeks. Right? I want a cheque in the post tomorrow morning. Otherwise . . .'

'Otherwise what?' Ferrari inquired mildly, eyeing the tinned carrots on an upper rack.

'I'll take you to court.'

'No, you won't, Mr Fletcher. You've enough on your plate.'

'Don't count on it. This friend I mentioned can be very persuasive.'

Gazing down at the contents of his trolley, Ferrari appeared to be calculating. 'Since you don't seem fully satisfied with the service . . .' he began.

'Let's get it straight, shall we? There hasn't been any service. You're a fake.'

'I'd like you to repeat that in front of a third party.'

'You heard it the first time.'

'If I were to offer a rebate, I'd be entitled to withhold such information as I've acquired.'

'That would be a shattering loss?' Fletcher demanded, after a pause.

The investigator shrugged, and waited.

Fletcher beckoned him to the checkout. With their

purchases transferred to carriers, the two of them made for the car park. Unlocking the door of a corroded Morris Maxi, Ferrari swung his carrier over to the rear seat, slipped the catch of the nearside door and motioned Fletcher to get in. Himself occuping the driver's seat, he lit a cigarette without offering the pack, inhaled deeply, sat back, blew smoke out of the open side-window.

'I may or may not,' he said at last, 'have kept tabs on your ex-spouse to your liking. But if you'll listen, I can tell you a thing or two concerning your kids.'

Fletcher's stomach lurched. 'What about them?'

'It's not specifically about them. It's the guy who's been watching them.'

'*What*? Who?'

'I never got around to asking his name,' Ferrari replied ironically, ejecting more smoke from the car. He scowled at the instrument panel. 'You might give me credit, Mr Fletcher, for a touch of expertise. I do have a record of some achievement, as it happens. I did serve in a city police force . . . and in case you're leaping to conclusions, I was *not* ousted for incompetence. I left, for personal reasons. You want to hear about this character, or not?'

'I want you to stop playing games. Tell me all you know.'

'What about our arrangement?'

'Assuming your facts are relevant, we can forget what I said.'

'Good enough.' Exposing an ashtray, Ferrari tapped his cigarette and rested his wrist on the wheel. 'For a couple of afternoons,' he recited, 'I kept a watching brief on your two youngsters, because I had an idea that what they did after school might be, um, relevant.' He lifted his eyebrows at Fletcher. 'I thought, if they showed signs of not bothering with the school bus, hanging about the playground, that kind of thing, it could indicate . . . Well, it might have implied that things weren't too settled at home, and I could have taken it from there. No luck, though. Normal routine each time. Except that on the second occasion . . .'

'What?'

'That was the afternoon I spotted the other car.'

'Mercedes?' Fletcher said keenly.

'No, it was a Sierra. Metallic-coffee job, with this thin-lipped type at the wheel. I'd noticed him as I arrived, parked in a side road along from the school. When the bus took off with the kids, he eased out and started to follow. That intrigued me.'

'So you kept him in sight?'

'All the way. He tailed the bus until it dropped off your pair at their gate, then puttered past the house while they went indoors. Then he turned and came back.'

'Was he sizing up the place?'

'Not exactly. I had the impression he was just getting his bearings.'

'What for?'

Ferrari spread his fingers. 'Some future occasion? You tell me. Anyway he drove off, back into town. He—'

'Did you follow?'

Ferrari slew him with a glance. 'When we got to the town centre,' he said deliberately, 'it dawned on him that he had a tail. He took off like a scalded cat, and after a few corners I lost him. You weren't paying me risk money,' he explained. 'And since I need this wagon for my livelihood, I wasn't inclined to chase him up the nearest lamp-post without good cause.'

'Did you get his number?'

'Checked it out later. Unless I got it wrong, there's no such number on record. So the plates could have been false. The car might have been stolen.'

'That's it, then? A man in a car drove past the house and looked at it.'

'One other thing. While he was parked near the school,

a copper on foot patrol came by, and as he was passing the Sierra I saw him bend down and talk to the guy through his window. I don't know what was said, but they had quite a chat.'

'What did he do—the policeman?'

'Nothing. Just strolled on. Whatever yarn the driver pitched him, he must have been satisfied.'

'Why mention it, then?'

'Just a point of interest,' said Ferrari, offended.

Fletcher ruminated. 'It didn't occur to you to let me know sooner about this? My kids could have been in danger.'

'If you'd known, what would you have done?'

'I could have alerted my ex.'

'And queered your own pitch?'

'How's that?'

'You hired me to get evidence of neglect. If you were going to put her on her guard, so that she took extra care and precautions . . .'

Fletcher shook his head in disbelief. 'The way you look at things, you should have aimed for the KGB, not the police. You might have gone far. We'd better do as I said, after all—terminate the contract. You can keep what you've already pocketed.'

'Thanks a lot. If you're getting out, I'll hand you your groceries.' As Fletcher reached back inside for the carrier, Ferrari held on. 'Just one thing. What made you ask if the car was a Merc?'

'Because that's the make of vehicle owned by someone my ex has been in contact with. Or so I'm given to understand. One can't be sure, of course. Informants,' Fletcher said tartly, capturing the bag, 'can be less than reliable.'

'You're well rid of him,' declared Eva.

'Maybe. His departure leaves a vacuum, though. Who

do we turn to now?'

'Ourselves. There's a lot to be said for it.'

Fletcher roamed restlessly while with deft movements she laid the table for four. Already he had noticed a difference in the house. Its faintly dusty complexion had been replaced by a sparkle. Flowering pot-plants had appeared on shelves and in alcoves. From the living-room fireplace, smokeless fuel was giving out a bright, companionable glow. The scent of roasting meat drifted from the kitchen. Halting to watch her, he said abruptly, 'You've been busy.'

Distributing cutlery, she lobbed him a smile. 'Children need a haven to come back to. Especially when . . . Were they surprised to find you waiting for them at the school?'

'Took it in their stride. They do most things. Apart from vanishing mothers.'

'Why did you?'

He glanced across from the hearthrug. 'Pick them up? For the moment, I just feel happier collecting them myself.'

Eva paused with knives clutched in her left fist. 'Why?'

'Because of what Ferrari told me.' He sketched the investigator's account. Eva stood with a palm planted on the table, a faint frown giving her face that paradoxically younger appearance which belied the maturity that seemed to take over at moments of restfulness. 'That,' she remarked eventually, laying out the knives, 'is certainly a trifle bothersome. But if the policeman spoke to this character . . .'

'I'm taking no chances.,'

'Quite right. You can use Louise's car, can't you? It's lying there idle.'

'I can't take her car. Without her permission, the insurance won't cover me.'

'Carry on using mine, then. I can manage without it. If I have to go into town, I'll take the bus.'

'Who could this car-lurker have been?' asked Fletcher, after an interval. 'Anything to do with Louise's disappearance, do you suppose?'

'In a way, I hope so.' Eva planked a jug of water on the centre of the table. 'But somehow I doubt it. I don't think he's significant at all. Just one of those gawpers with time on their hands. Will you call the children, love? Make sure they've washed their hands. We'll have supper early, in case that Sergeant Dawson turns up again with more questions.'

Promptly at seven-thirty the sergeant appeared on the doorstep. Fletcher took him into the large, cheerless breakfast-room at the front of the house and offered whisky, which was accepted. 'Nippy tonight,' remarked Dawson, downing his drink with relish. 'Never was wild about March. Half-and-half time of year, if you ask me. Can't decide if it's winter or spring. So, where's this lady, Mr Fletcher, who's gone AWOL? Any ideas?'

'Sergeant, if I had . . .'

'You'd be phoning her to come back, hot-foot, and look after her family.' Sergeant Dawson said it cheerily. A beefy, ruddy-faced man in his middle thirties, he was the epitome of the bluff country cop with a yokel manner disguising, Fletcher sensed, more than a streak of keen intelligence. 'Lucky for them you've got Mrs Maynard to cook and polish for a bit. Known her a while, have you?'

'She's an office colleague of mine. Very kindly, she offered to step into the breach.'

'What happens when she can't spare the time any more?'

'We'll face that problem when it arises.'

'One obstacle at a time, eh? Good thinking. Mrs Fletcher could be back by tomorrow, of course.' The sergeant added suddenly, 'Think she might be?'

'I wish I knew.'

Dawson wandered to the window. 'We've checked on

the names and places you gave us,' he volunteered, peering out at the darkness. 'Not much from any of 'em. Leaving aside Miss Sally Wentworth, who was quite helpful. Know her yourself, do you?'

'Not by sight. We spoke on the phone last night for the first time.'

'That so? Can't say the same as to her and Mrs Fletcher. Them two had been chewing the fat together, and no mistake.'

'What do you mean?'

Dawson turned to examine him in evident faint surprise. 'I mean, your ex seems to have been giving Miss Wentworth the lowdown on her personal life, which ought to be useful from our point of view . . . but is it?'

'I don't know. Isn't it?'

Draining his Scotch, the sergeant eyed the empty glass with some regret but declined with uplifted hand the offer of a refill. 'Remains to be seen, sir, I'd say. Mrs Fletcher apparently had been full of this male acquaintance she'd just met. You'd not heard about him?'

'Miss Wentworth mentioned him last night. Mr Rosenberg.'

'That's the fella. Seems it was one of those contrived meetings via the . . . You knew about that?'

'I guessed.'

Prowling the room, Dawson halted in front of a watercolour representing a harbour, with ships' masts against an evening sky, and bent an appraising eye upon its composition. 'Swept a bit off her feet, Mrs Fletcher was, by all accounts. According to Miss Wentworth, he'd taken her to lunch at some swank restaurant, then bought her a couple of fancy outfits from a dress em-por-i-um . . . no expense spared, you might say. And when Miss Wentworth last spoke to her, she was looking ahead to the time when these dresses were to be delivered and . . .'

The sergeant paused. 'And one would assume,' he

added severely, 'put to some appropriate use. All of which adds up to something, I reckon you'll agree.'

'It adds up to the obvious fact,' Fletcher said stonily, 'that my former wife has been bowled over by someone brandishing a cheque-book . . . which doesn't altogether startle me. The question is, who and where is Mr Rosenberg?'

'Aha.' Dawson swung about. 'There lies a possible solution, if we knew those answers. We've made some inquiries. Martelli's, where they lunched—they know Mr Rosenberg all right, but as for knowing anything *about* him . . . He's just a face they've seen a few times. A customer with banknotes to chuck around. No help there. Then there's the dress shop, Rosalind's at Cheltenham. We've asked for an inquiry to be made there, but the same probably applies. If he paid cash, like he did at Martelli's, we've nothing to go on. So—just who *is* Mr Rosenberg?'

'If Louise is with him,' suggested Fletcher, 'and he's not aware she's walked out on her own children . . . might he respond to publicity?'

'It's possible. We're planning to release details to the Press tomorrow. You're prepared for that?'

'Go right ahead.'

'Mind you, we could be entirely on the wrong tack. Her disappearance might have nothing whatever to do with him.'

'I doubt that. Mrs Willerby next door saw her go off in this large, chauffeur-driven car. It adds up.'

'Looks like it, sir.' Sergeant Dawson gave him a sad, worldly smile, shook his head ponderously, twice, then became galvanized by a new, crisp purposefulness. 'Well now. A few routine questions I have to put to you . . .'

'Has he gone?' asked Eva, on Fletcher's return to the kitchen.

'For the moment. He's going to give the story to the

Press, in the hope that this Rosenberg comes forward.'

'Sounds like sense.'

His nod was pensive. 'We'll see.'

CHAPTER 8

The dormer window was high in the sloped ceiling. By dragging the table beneath it and swarming up, Louise was just able to see through the lowest pane. Fields, trees, hedgerows, cattle-fencing. No other habitation was in sight.

Climbing down, she returned to the bed and picked up one of the half-dozen copies of *Woman*, opening it at random to a picture of a knitted yellow short dress worn by a peach-faced girl with a mocking smile. She studied it blankly, her mind elsewhere.

Her throat was sore from shouting. Her knuckles were grazed and bruised. The attic door had not even quivered to her pounding. The window was a non-starter. Disregarding the fact that the room was at roof-level, the metal bars fixed across the windowframe were mere inches apart, solidly screwed in at both ends.

Her discomfort during the hours of darkness had been largely of the mental kind. The bed in which she had regained consciousness was well-sprung, adequately equipped with blankets and linen. The room itself was reasonably warm. Already she knew it intimately, every angle and crevice. During the small hours she had explored it ragingly, hunting for a single weak spot, grizzling to herself.

Hurling the magazine into a corner, she dragged herself off the bed and carried the electric kettle from the table into the tiny bathroom built into one end of the attic. She felt queasy inside. Having refilled the kettle, she brought it back, plugged in, switched on. She crammed a teabag into the tin pot that stood on a plastic tray, along with a blue and white cup and saucer and a stainless steel jug of milk, covered with cling-film. On a corner of the table stood a plastic box containing two-thirds of a white sliced loaf: beneath the table, an electric toaster was connected by means of an adaptor to the same socket that fed the kettle. Butter was available in an insulated dish.

The idea of food was repulsive. Drink . . . that was another matter. Stimulation was what she needed. What had happened to her was so outrageous, so incredible, that violent reaction should have been easy; and yet it was proving to be nothing of the kind. After her initial outburst upon awaking, the temptation had been to sink, to snivel. She was damned if she was going to yield to that.

In that case, maybe she should eat? With a feeling of nuasea she took two bread slices from the container, dropped them into the toaster slots, pressed them down. Then she made tea.

From the edge of the mattress, as she sipped, she surveyed the attic in the light of a pallid dawn.

The room occupied a length of perhaps twenty feet and a width of ten beneath a raftered and plastered ceiling pitched on three sides, merging into cream-emulsioned walls that bulged here and there as if trying with limited success to conceal multiple pregnancies. The modernization that had been carried out was itself of some antiquity, to judge from the flaking paintwork, the stained carpeting, the chipped and less than slimline radiator fitments. The single door, opposite the window, was flush-fitting, with an aluminium lever handle that responded to downward pressure but failed to release the catch.

The bathroom, formed by a chipboard partition, was

equipped with a pale green suite of vitreous enamel bearing marks of heavy discoloration around the plugholes. The flush toilet operated with groaning reluctance. As attic conversions went, it was serviceable if makeshift. As a prison, it was secure.

Since regaining her faculties, Louise had heard nothing except, at about seven-fifteen, the brief echoing mutter of a car engine from below the window. After it had dwindled and died, complete silence had persisted. It was now eight-thirty. Suddenly infuriated by the inactivity, Louise left her tea half-drunk while she clambered back on to the table and stood on tiptoe, striving to gain a fresh angle of vision through the panes but thwarted by the bars. For want of a choice, she inspected them.

Their installation, she inferred, was recent. Each steel tube, untarnished, was held by screws whose burred heads were still shiny. Using her nail-file, could she yank them out?

Hopeless as the task was, for the sake of something to do she made the effort. When her fingers could take no more of it, she stopped. Binding a gash with her handkerchief, she returned to the floor, nursing the pain, glaring impotently at the locked door. Next to her feet, unnoticed, the tanned slices had shot up from the toaster. She had forgotten about eating.

She gathered breath in her lungs. 'Hey! Anybody around?'

The cry scoured her throat. Coughing weakly, she moved towards the varnished wooden chair that stood against the wall at the foot of the bed: apart from the table, it was the sole other item of furniture in the room. Seizing it, she took it across to the door.

The noise of timber against timber was duller than she had hoped. Before long the legs parted company with the seat. The backrest followed. Exhausted, she swung the individual pieces a few more times before scattering them over the carpet. Staggering back to the bed, she collapsed face down, weeping breathlessly in rage and frustration. Presently, feeling sick, she rose and made for the bathroom.

With agonizing slowness, Terri was crawling through the window with Kevin in pursuit. Louise herself was behind and below, trying vainly to shout encouragement.

She stretched upwards. Instead of making contact with Terri's trailing foot, she felt herself toppling against the wall-base. There was no impact. Merely a wallowing sensation, as if the brickwork were foam rubber. Both children had vanished. Gripped by a deadly fear, fighting for equilibrium, she let out a gasp, a strangled cry, and heard the throbbing note of a motor.

Heart palpitating, she lay still on the mattress, listening to the sound from outside.

The suffocating residue of the dream was hard to shake off. The children, she felt, must be near at hand, struggling to reach her or to escape; calling for her. The car engine gave a louder growl, and cut out. A door slammed.

Feet clumped across concrete. In sudden hope, she sat up.

The room swam, circled. Shutting her eyes, she waited briefly before reopening them to consult her watch. Nine-fifty. The tea remaining in the cup was cold sludge. Had she slept all day?

If so, it would have been dark again. She had dozed merely for an hour or so. The sun had emerged: its rays slanted through the glass to strike the opposite wall. She still felt a little sick. If she tried to stand, the floor unquestionably would rise to meet her. There was no point in getting on her feet. She had tried all that.

Footfalls shook the staircase. Almost in apathy she sat

mentally charting their progress, heard them change cadence, presumably at a midway landing, before resuming their steady ascent to attic-level. Outside the door they paused, A tinkling reached her ears. The sliding of metal. She sat without breathing, fingers clenched on the bedclothes.

The inward swing of the door heralded another pause. The figure in the doorway stood motionless for a second or two, inspecting her: then it came three paces into the room. She stared, breathing strenuously in a futile attempt to arrest the spinning of her head.

'So it's you,' she heard herself say. 'Scott said you were ill. Where's Mr Rosenberg?'

'I hope you slept well.' The remark lacked sincerity. He stood with pocketed hands, looking down at her, his only apparent emotion one of faint curiosity. She gazed at him listlessly.

'You've left off your peaked cap.'

'I don't need it any more. I stopped being Jackson some days ago.'

'So who are you now?'

His glanced wandered to the two untouched slices in the toaster. 'Our catering not agreeing with you?'

'I've not sampled it. Whose crazy idea was this? Rosenberg's? If so, he's going to regret it, I can tell you.'

Jackson went and leaned against the wall, watching her. He looked as dour, as impenetrable as he had when driving them to Cheltenham and back: the sole difference was that, in place of his chauffeur's uniform, he was now clad informally in leather jacket and cords. Louise began to find his silent scrutiny unnerving. She tried once more. 'Is he here?'

'Rosenberg? You don't want to bother yourself about him.'

'That's good to know. What should I be bothering myself about?'

Her sarcasm was self-defeating. Nothing she said seemed to make the smallest impact upon this sandy-haired creature with the cold eyes that continued to study her as though she were a none-too-likeable puppy that needed correction. Unable to remain still, she swung her legs out from the bed, pushed herself upright, lost balance, reeled into the centre of the room. Dimly, through a fog, she was aware of Jackson moving with celerity back towards the door, stationing himself to block the exit. Humiliated, she groped her way back to the bed, sat heavily, clutched her head with both hands.

'Don't panic on my account,' she mumbled. 'I'm in no shape to try anything.'

'I know.'

The assurance of the statement shot ice into her veins. She said dully, 'Was it the milk? Did you add something?'

'All you're suffering from is a hangover from the chloroform. It'll pass.'

'*Chloroform?*' She thought back, to the moment of arrival. A farmyard entrance. A struggle. A hand descending . . . 'Is that what that moron used on me? What is this—a ransom job? You must be out of your minds. I don't have two pennies to rub together.'

'But you do have two children.'

The ice became a deadweight mass, crushing her down. 'What about them? What do they have to do with anything?'

Once more Jackson directed his gaze at the toaster. 'If you don't care for bread, we can bring you a boiled egg. Helps settle the stomach.'

'What was that crack about my children? What are you getting at?'

'One soft-boiled egg, coming up.' Backing to the far side of the door, he closed it and activated the lock. The staircase shook under his descending tread. Another door thumped distantly as a forerunner of silence.

'Come back here!' Her voice was cracked, falsetto, a ludicrous irrelevance. 'I insist that you answer me. Do you hear?'

Her right foot kicked the toaster. Snatching it up, she wrenched it from its flex and hurled it at the window bars. Rebounding, it fell back to the carpet, bounced, came to rest partly beneath the bed. With a sob at her throat, Louise glared around. Baulked, she darted into the bathroom, seized the bar of soap from the dish, returned with it, took aim, flung it with all her strength. By chance, it passed between two of the steel bars to continue unchecked through a pane, taking out shards in an explosion of noise. A jagged space marked its passage.

Instantly a cool draught made itself felt. Having stared for a moment at the damage, Louise threw herself back on to the bed and beat impotently at the springs. After a while, from pure fatigue, she quietened. She lay thinking.

This time the footfalls on the staircase were slower, more measured, as though something was being carried.

Outside the door, they paused. There was the faint sound of a burden being deposited upon floorboards, followed by the scrape of a key in the lock. A second pause. An interlude of scuffing. With a click, the door started to open.

The leading edge of a tray appeared first. The pursuing head and shoulders came only inches beyond the line of the door-lintel before hesitating. From her elevated position on the table behind the door, Louise couldn't see the eyes but she knew they were directed at the empty bed opposite: she knew also that they would not be for long. The angle was awkward but it had to be now. Gritting her teeth, she brought the chairleg down, hard.

Although the blow was a glancing one, the impact was solid enough to jar her arm. More important, it produced a half-throttled grunt, then a crash as the tray hit the floor, strewing its contents. In its wake, the bearer slumped to his knees, stayed briefly in that posture as though examining the nap of the carpet, and finally fell on his side. Dropping the chairleg, Louise leapt down, gasping as she landed, half-toppling. She recovered her footing. Jumping over the inert figure, she ran out to the landing.

The stairs went off to the left, Uncarpeted, steep and unlit, they were equipped with a wooden handrail which, under her weight, tore free of the wall at the bottom end as she descended. Sprawling full-length on the lower landing, she rolled over to collide painfully with a balustrade. Moaning, she dragged herself up. The steps of the second flight were shallower, better lit. As she stumbled down, she heard a faint call from above.

The impetus of her arrival at ground-floor level impelled her along the hallway in the direction she least wanted, away from the glazed outer door. Pulling up, she wheeled and headed back, striving to quicken her limbs, feeling them resist her as if she had just run a marathon. Reaching the door, she fell upon the latch.

It yielded readily. Obeying the drag of her arms, the door swung wide to display a sunlit morning, a paved yard, quarrystone walls. Away to the right, near a hydrant, a metallic-brown saloon was parked with its nose to a gateway. She began making for it: then, torn by uncertainty, she veered and headed for the opening. Her thin, heeled shoes skittered on the flagstones. A frigid breeze thwacked into her, robbing her of breath.

Beyond the gateway, outhouses bordered each flank of the ribbed-concrete track which led to the second gate, with its cattle-grid. Past this, the surface became asphalt which ran some distance uphill to the crest. Wire fencing and a ditch skirted the track on each side.

How far to the road? In the Mercedes, the distance had

seemed nothing. Legs were not wheels. Her calves felt rubbery, powerless. Toiling between the outhouses, she was unable to silence the clatter of her heels. From a barn, an unseen cow released a sudden bellow, sending her heart into her throat. Her chest began to tighten.

She was nearing the second gate when the self-starter whirred behind her.

The urge to turn and look was overwhelming. Run, she told herself. Ignore the drumming in the ears. Think of the children. Think of the next ten yards, the next five steps. The gate loomed. And, with it, the grid. There was no way to by-pass it: barbed wire ran to both gateposts. Slowing, she started to pick her way across. She was almost at the far side when she lost a shoe.

Gaining the asphalt, she lurched one-sidedly for a yard or two before kicking off the other shoe and continuing in stockinged feet. A surface bulge caught her unawares. She stubbed a toe, cried out in pain, hopped, hobbled. From close behind, there was a roaring sound. Something went past her, so close that it brushed her hip. Exhaust fumes stung her nostrils.

Involuntarily she reeled at a tangent towards the right-hand ditch. She tried to arrest herself: then at the last instant she tried to jump. The bank on the farther side sprang towards her. Her mouth filled with soft earth.

Dazed, she felt herself lifted. Upholstery was embracing her, and yet despite its support she was being flung about. The corrugated roofs of the outhouses bobbed back into view. Alongside her, somebody was talking. She did her best to listen, to comprehend.

'. . . one more time,' the voice was saying, 'and we'll have to revise our approach. You'll leave us no option.'

'Option?' Amazingly, her own voice still functioned. 'What choice have you given me? What did you expect?'

'I never expected violence.' Applying the handbrake viciously, Jackson twisted in his seat to regard her with a new intensity. 'Maybe I should have.'

'If you thought I was going to sit there tamely, you must be cuckoo.' Louise wiped her lips with a rag she had found in a pocket of the car. The soil she had half-swallowed was gritty about her teeth.

'I should have known what you were like. I should have been prepared.'

'What *I'm* like?' She stared back in dull incredulity. 'Who's the one being manhandled around here? Who's being locked up, for no reason? How do you think I—'

'Shut up.' He said it dispassionately, not raising his voice.

For some reason she complied. The paralysis of terror was creeping up on her. She was beginning to feel like the unwitting subject of some inhuman experiment that was commencing to give false readings, to the vexation of its sponsors. Whatever she said seemed to compound the annoyance. And yet it was she, surely, who was the injured party?

Of course she was. It was important, crucial, to keep that rigidly in mind. Against her will she was being held, without explanation, and there were no men in white coats padding around to furnish a possible clue. Merely this man, clad in country attire and a remote facial expression; plus another, whose face she had yet to inspect. Never before had she hit anyone. She hoped he bled easily.

Jackson edged into her train of thought. 'Did you have to slug my partner so hard? What good did it do?'

'Frankly, it did me a power of good.'

He nodded. 'It figures. Enjoy clobbering men, don't you?' Leaning past her, he shoved open the nearside door. 'Get out.'

The flagstones were cold against her shoeless feet. Limply, all fight knocked out of her, she obeyed his prodding gesture and set off back towards the farmhouse, drained of mental resource. Clearly sceptical of her docility, Jackson kept close at her shoulder, both hands swinging free, at red alert. The house, she noted cloudily, was rectangular, brick and tile with a slated roof from which the dormer window jutted like a cannon-hatch, flaunting its shattered pane. Next to her ear, Jackson said, 'You're going to find it draughty from now on. You've only yourself to blame.'

Disdaining to reply, she preceded him into the house. The hapless Scott was slumped on a hall chair with a handkerchief pressed to his scalp. He gave her an eloquent glance as they passed, but said nothing. Jackson jerked a thumb.

'Get yourself cleaned up through there. You'll find some brandy in one of the cupboards.' As they climbed the stairs, Scott was rising groggily and making for a door at the rear.

'I'm *not* a violent person,' Louise, close to tears, told Jackson on the first landing. 'But put yourself in my place. I'm a prisoner . . . a hostage . . . what? I'm blocked off from the world. I keep hearing vague threats. Can you blame me for cutting loose?'

He nudged her upwards. At the top, she turned to confront him again. 'Look, you're not going to harm my children, are you?' Her voice was threatening to give out. She dragged in a breath. 'That's all I want to know. I'll stay here, gladly, if you tell me they're going to be all right. *Please*.'

The door to the attic stood open. He motioned her inside. As she started to turn, with a fresh appeal on her lips, the door clapped shut in her face.

CHAPTER 9

'We're simply checking,' explained the social worker, 'to make quite certain that Kevin and, um . . .'

'Terri.'

'Terri, yes. To establish that they're both going to be properly looked after, on a permanent basis, now that their mother seems to be . . .'

'No longer concerned with them,' suggested Eva, bringing two cups of coffee to the kitchen table.

'Not quite positive yet, is it? But it certainly begins to look rather as if . . .'

The sentence hung unfinished, yet again. Seating herself opposite the social worker, an earnest young woman peering through square-rimmed spectacles, Eva proffered the sugar bowl and watched her stir in a spoonful and a half. She said, 'They're super kids.'

'How long is it now, Mrs Maynard, you've been looking after them?'

'Three days. Since Mrs Fletcher . . . went missing.'

'How do you manage? I understand you're a working lady.'

'I've just handed in my notice. I was only working for the sake of having something to do, actually. Now that I've taken this on, it's not necessary.'

'Finance?'

'Mr Fletcher and I have come to an arrangement.'

'What if Mrs Fletcher comes back?'

'We'll think about that if it happens.' Eva sipped thoughtfully at her coffee. 'Assuming she did, and it turned out she'd been away of her own free will, what attitude do you think the authorities . . . ?'

'Difficult to say.' The social worker looked profound.

'Obviously it would depend on the circumstances. Reasons for her absence and so forth. If it wasn't unavoidable, I think there'd have to be a reassessment. We couldn't have young children left with someone so unreliable.' The social worker buried her face in her cup, then came up with a small gasp for air. 'The husband, Mr Fletcher. Ex-husband, I should say. Fond of the youngsters, is he?'

'They're his life.'

The young woman scribbled something on a notepad. She glanced around the kitchen. 'All looks beautifully neat in here. You must have been working very hard, Mrs Maynard.'

'I like everything to be nice for them. They're bound to be feeling a bit lost and insecure just now. We're trying to give them back some stability.'

The social worker beamed through her spectacles. 'Lucky pair.'

After she had gone, Eva washed and dried the crockery, packed laundry into a plastic bag and caught the bus into town. While the garments were being tortured in the Laundromat she did some essential shopping before entering the Farmhouse Tearoom for a snack in place of lunch. The place was crowded and she had to share a table. Her companion, a square-faced woman with mousy-brown hair, was dealing with a glass of lemon tea and a wholemeal scone. Eva murmured an apology for intruding.

'Not at all,' the woman assured her. 'It's not often so packed in here.'

'Anyway I shan't be long.' Eva ordered an egg on toast from a hunted waitress. 'I have to go back for my laundry, before someone hauls it out of the machine and wipes the floor with it.'

The woman smiled. 'I have my own machine, luckily.'

'So do I. But it's a type I've not met before and we have

to get acquainted. So I thought I'd get this lot done while I shopped.'

'You've a family?'

'I'm caring for a couple of children while their mother's away.'

The woman showed interest. 'You're a foster-parent?'

'Just helping out a friend.' Unfurling her newspaper, Eva scanned the headlines.

The woman's voice penetrated the newsprint. 'The friend's name wouldn't happen to be Fletcher, by any chance?'

Eva looked up. 'However did you know?'

'Just a guess. Louise Fletcher—the one who's missing. I know her quite well.'

Eva lowered the newspaper. 'You're not Sally . . . Sally . . . ?'

'Wentworth. That's it, that's who I am. Colin phoned me the other night, as you probably know. Asking if I could shed any light on Louise's disappearance.'

Shrugging off her coat, Eva secured it to the back of her chair. 'Which you couldn't?'

'It's an utter mystery. But as I told Colin, I feel it has something to do with this man.'

'The one she's supposed to have met? Yes, Col . . . Mr Fletcher told me. Seems feasible. Though I find it extraordinary that any woman could . . .' Eva paused. 'I don't know Mrs Fletcher personally, of course. You'd be better placed to give an opinion.'

'One doesn't like to speculate,' Sally said gently. 'How are the children, by the way?'

'Bewildered. Otherwise fine.'

'Colin's fortunate to have you around.' Collecting her gloves Sally scraped back her chair. 'Well, I simply must be off. Do give Colin my . . . Tell him if there's anything I can do, he's not to hesitate to ring. You'll be around for a while yet, I take it?'

'At least until Mrs Fletcher reappears. At their age, the children need somebody feminine.'

'Of course they do. I'm sorry, I didn't ask your name . . .'

'Mrs Maynard.'

'So pleased to have met you. Carry on the good work.'

Eva watched her thread her way out between tables. When her egg on toast arrived, she ate it quickly before making her way back to the Laundromat. Having collected and dried the washing, she was in time for the two-thirty bus home.

On his arrival with the children, Fletcher seemed preoccupied. Asking no questions, Eva provided a welcome that was low-key but cheerful, giving extra attention to Terri: the child was even quieter than usual, a shade withdrawn. Neither of them asked about their mother. Having allocated them a couple of specially-hoarded tasks in the kitchen, Eva took a medium sherry to Fletcher in the living-room. He accepted it with a short-lived smile of thanks. 'Not having one?'

'Later.' Perching next to him on the chair-arm, she removed the spectacles from his nose and began polishing them with a tissue. 'I don't want to sound like the little homebody, but you look flopped out. You really do.'

'I'm worried about Louise.'

She waited a moment. 'Naturally you are. It's hard to make plans when—'

'I don't mean that.' He glanced up, spilling sherry over the cushion with an unguarded movement of his arm. 'It's Louise herself. We had our ups and downs, God knows, but the more I think about it, the more I'm convinced . . . I just *know* she'd never do a thing like this. Not from choice.'

Eva stared into the fire. 'If something had happened to her,' she said presently, 'how would you honestly feel about it? Personally, that is.'

'*If something had happened.*' He repeated the phrase slowly. 'I'm never entirely certain what's meant by that.'

'If she was never going to come back.'

'I'd prefer to shelve the topic.'

'Why?'

His head jolted slightly. 'Odd question. What am I supposed to do—hope she stays away?'

'It would solve a lot of problems.'

'I don't think you quite understand. If she were never to show up . . .'

'Yes?'

'Think of the effect it would have on those two outside. How could one ever explain it to them?'

'They'd come to terms,' Eva said practically. 'Kids do. As long as they had plenty of alternative affection . . . which they would have.'

'I hope you're right.'

Pocketing the tissue, Eva looped the spectacles back on to his ears. 'After three days' experience of your pair,' she remarked, 'I feel entitled to an opinion. Besides . . .' She hesitated, then went on. 'I'm not sure I follow your argument. You wanted to get them away from Louise, didn't you? That was the whole idea. Now that it seems possible, you're not—'

'I never wanted it to happen like this.'

'Then how?'

Fletcher made an indecisive gesture. She added, 'By a court order? All nicely legal and above board? I doubt if either Kevin or Terri would take particular note of the difference. Whichever way it occurs, they're going to have to adapt.'

'But never knowing just what's become of her . . .'

'Is it them, Colin, you're mainly concerned for? Or yourself?'

His body gave a jerk. After an interval he said on a note of subdued obstinacy, 'When you've been married to a person, you can't just rinse them away down some forgotten wastepipe.'

'I understand that.' She watched him carefully. 'I still think, though, you're fretting over nothing. Louise can take care of herself. Isn't that about all she's ever done?' Rising, she scooped fuel from the bucket and threw it on the open fire, deadening the glow. 'I met someone today, in the town.'

'Who?'

'That friend of Louise's. Sally Wentworth. We had quite a chat.'

'I didn't know you were acquainted.'

'We weren't. We got talking by chance, in a café.'

Fletcher sat up. 'She'd not heard anything?'

'No. But I got the impression she'd drawn her own conclusions.'

'Meaning?'

Eva returned to her perch. 'Surely it's obvious. Like us, she feels that this man Rosenberg must have something to do with it. She didn't say so, but she suspects that Louise has gone off with him.'

'More invaluable testimony,' Fletcher said, without expression. 'What did you think of her?'

'Sally Wentworth? She seems a very . . . Yes, darling, what is it?'

Terri had appeared silently at the door. Addressing her father, she said, 'We can't find any matches.'

'They should be in the . . . Hold on, I'll be out.' Wordlessly the child withdrew. Rising, Eva added sedatively to Fletcher, 'Don't agonize over Louise. She's fine, I'm certain. Having a high old time, probably, in the knowledge that the kids are being taken care of meanwhile. I know her sort. I told you, didn't I? We've had personal experience in the family.'

'We do have one report,' said Detective-Inspector Leslie

Cummings, shuffling papers on his desk, 'of a medium to large car, *possibly* a Merc, being driven east along the Oxford road, *possibly* with a rear passenger who might *possibly* have been a youngish woman answering vaguely to Mrs Fletcher's description . . .'

'Sounds like a giant stride.'

'Well, sir, I won't deny that the source of the information lacks pedigree. One Harry Packer, bartender at the Stag and Bullfinch. He told us he was cleaning the saloon bar windows when he caught a glimpse of this outfit as it hummed past. Old Harry, he enjoys the spotlight. And I dare say he'd been reading the newspapers. But he could genuinely have seen your ex-wife, you can't dismiss him out of hand.'

'I wouldn't want to,' said Fletcher. 'Did he offer an opinion as to the . . . condition of the passenger?'

Cummings frowned at his notes. 'Says he thought she was sitting "quite peaceable-like". That rings true. If she hadn't been, presumably he'd have told us like a shot. Other than that, sir . . .' The inspector straightened up. 'I can't say we've had an almighty response to our inquiries. The computer did throw up a couple of Rosenbergs, both owners of Mercedes cars. Copper-bottomed alibi in each case: no help there. Nil result from car-hire firms. Oh, and nothing from the dress shop at Cheltenham. As we surmised, he settled in cash, this mystery individual, and there's damn-all else they know about him. Can't even agree on a description. Aside from Harry, nobody's reacted to the publicity as far as we're concerned. How about your end?'

'We've had a local reporter at the door, plus one or two phone calls that got us nowhere. Now it seems to have tailed off. The media don't seem that interested.'

'Just another missing housewife,' Cummings agreed with an air of realism. 'Ex-wife, rather.' He caught Fletcher's eye. 'Saving a bit on maintenance, sir, if that's a consolation. Dare say you were finding it a drag on your resources.'

'I'm still looking after my children,' Fletcher replied glacially. 'Not to mention the house. I wouldn't call that a cash bonus.'

'Point taken.' The inspector mused. Then glanced up. 'Well, Mr Fletcher, I'm obliged to you for calling in. Any developments, we'll keep you informed. And if you should learn anything yourself . . . Grand. Goodbye for now.'

Late in reaching the office, Fletcher fended off the perfunctory polite inquiries from the girls before turning his remaining energies to the elimination of the backlog accumulating in his in-tray. More than ever, he felt unsettled. The children were starting to worry him. At home, both of them seemed unnaturally quiet and constrained: cooperative, and yet remote. They reminded him of a pair of motorists, each steering cautiously after a long day's drive for fear of a roadblock. How, inwardly, were they reacting to the situation? He yearned to ask them, but he didn't know how. He stared bleakly at the mail-stack. Concentration was a problem. To focus his mind, he slit open a few envelopes. As he was shaking the contents from the first, his telephone burped.

'Can you spare half an hour? Any time today.'

Fletcher kept his voice in check. 'I thought I'd paid you off.'

'I've something that might interest you.'

'That's pretty vague. What if I say no?'

'Up to you. If you feel like passing up a possibility . . .'

Fletcher glanced at his watch. 'I'll meet you—without obligation, understood? Make it the Wimpy Bar in Percival Street. Ten minutes.' Hanging up, he added to the room at large, 'I'm off out again. Urgent business. If anyone calls, say I'll be back at eleven.'

'Right you are, Mr Fletcher.'

The Wimpy Bar had the forlorn aspect of a ski resort out of season. Arriving three minutes late, Ferrari brought across a black coffee and occupied the seat opposite Fletcher's, inhaled lingeringly, patted his mouth with a sleeve, settled back. He wore a self-confident air, like an ill-fitting sweater.

'Information,' he said tersely. 'Outline first: then if you want to invest, the full works. Okay?'

'Go ahead.'

'What if I were to tell you I've traced the ownership of that Sierra I was telling you about?'

Fletcher eyed him steadily. 'What if you were?'

'Also, that I know the guy.'

'Keep talking.'

A headshake came from the investigator. 'Charitable causes aren't my pitch.' He fingered his cup.

Fletcher cogitated. 'Twenty quid,' he said finally. 'Half now, half when you've told me.'

'Thirty.'

'I'm tight on cash.'

'Who isn't? Chasing up this case has cost me, I can tell you.'

'I told you to drop it.'

'You forget, I'm a pro. Leaving jobs half-done irritates me.'

'Twenty-five. Ten now, the rest afterwards.' Fletcher took out his wallet, passed across a banknote. 'Let's have it. Who is he?'

'His name's Steve Bradley,' said Ferrari, folding the advance away. 'Alias Clark; alias Scott; alias you-name-it. As you may gather from that, he's got previous. I ran up against him a couple of times, when I was in uniform. Small-time operator. A bit of goods-handling, a spot of wheelmanship, the odd con-trick. Not rough, but not particular either.'

'If you've met him before, why didn't you recognize him?'

'He's changed,' said Ferrari, aggrieved. 'Thinner in the face, and he's lost some hair. And I only saw him from a distance, don't forget.'

'So how can you be sure it was him?'

Ferrari drooped an eyelid. 'I do have a few Fuzz connections. That's how I traced the Sierra. The copper who had a word with him—'

'I thought you said the number-plates were false?'

'I said they might be. That's because I misread the number. If you want the complete truth,' Ferrari added defensively, 'my eyesight's not what it was.'

Fletcher sighed. 'I suppose it was like my current luck to saddle me with a private eye who's short-sighted. This Steve Bradley, then. Is he up to something?'

'Let me just tell you what I dug out. The beat copper who spoke to him had made a note of the Sierra's registration, of course. He was interested enough later to check with the computer. Up came Bradley's name. The mere fact that he was on file prompted a few discreet inquiries, but nothing much came of them. Bradley was living—is living—in rooms just outside Abingmore, and working for a roofing contractor. Part of his job, apparently, is to scout out likely buildings for repair, which, as he explained to the copper on patrol, accounted for his interest in the school. Its roof *is* in bad shape, no question.'

'His story holds water, then?'

'Up to a point. His boss confirmed that he has this roving commission to drum up contracts.'

'So why have I handed over ten quid to be told this?'

'There's more.'

'Right, let's hear it. Another of Bradley's aliases is Rosenberg? Is that what you're going to tell me?'

'From my inquiries,' Ferrari said deliberately, clearly

disapproving of the pace, 'there's no visible link between Bradley and this Rosenberg we keep hearing about. In any case, Bradley's hardly the type. I doubt if he'd be capable of posing as a smooth, moneyed charmer. Not his scene at all.'

'He's a con man, you said.'

'Not in that category. Three-card trick stuff.'

'Let's just recap,' suggested Fletcher after a pause. 'A small-time crook by the name of Bradley—or Scott, or whatever he chooses to call himself—was seen by you watching the school. You then saw him tail the school bus to my ex-wife's house and give it the once-over. Since then you've not seen him around Bancester, but you find that he does have a valid reason for looking at buildings. Right?'

'Correct.'

'Not much, is it? Any connection with my affairs seems a bit tenuous. What's this "more" you were mentioning?'

Ferrari leaned forward. 'I'll tell you,' he said.

CHAPTER 10

Splinters of moisture stung her out of sleep. Sitting up, she stared for a moment into the darkness, hearing a moan of wind in trees, the spasmodic clatter of rain against glass. Somewhere outside, a gate was being blown repeatedly against its retaining post.

More droplets showered her. Crawling out of bed, she switched on the light, peered up at the hole in the pane. The rag that had been stuffed into it was hanging from one of the bars. Shivering, she dragged the table along, swarmed up, repacked the hole, gasped a little as the gale attacked her throat. Returning to the floor, she wrapped herself in her coat before plugging in the electric kettle and switching on.

The knock came as she was toasting a slice of bread. Walking across to the door, she said, 'What do you want?'

'Pull the door open.'

With a shrug, she did as she was ordered. Both of them were standing there, Jackson slightly to the fore. Scott had a towel-wrapped broom handle in his grasp. She stood hand on hip, looking at them. 'Taking no chances, are you?'

Jackson stepped into the room. Behind him, Scott drew the door shut and left himself and the broom handle outside on the landing. Returning to the bed, Louise sat on the edge, captured the freshly toasted slice, added a dob of butter and bit into it noisily. Jackson watched without emotion.

'New toaster working all right?'

'What do you care?'

'We like things in good order around here.'

'In that case, you might consider replacing that pane of glass. The weather's getting in.'

'You smashed it.'

'Oh, I do apologize. I must remember to take better care of my cell.'

Pocketing his hands, Jackson leaned against the wall to observe her. She took another loud, defiant mouthful of toast. 'That seems to be a favourite pose of yours. Get a kick out of it?'

'No.' The expressionless eyes didn't blink.

'When are you thinking of explaining all this?'

He said nothing.

'You get some kind of a thrill out of it. Right? Some female turned you down, so I'm the revenge-substitute. Is that it?'

'You flatter yourself.'

'If that's what you think, you don't know me at all.'

'I know all I need to.'

'Really? I hadn't appreciated my fame was spreading.' The note of cutting sarcasm was getting harder to sustain. There was more to this dialogue than she could discern: the deadening dismay that was taking a grip of her was becoming impossible to mask. She launched a last-ditch attempt. 'In Bancester, was it? You've seen me around? Did I snub you, without realizing it? Just tell me. We can come to an understanding.'

Jackson stood relaxed against the wall. 'I don't need an understanding.'

Regardless of the crumbs and butter-smears clinging to her fingers, Louise thrust them distractedly through her hair. 'What baffles me,' she said shakily, after a pause, 'is why you're troubling to come up and see me at all. Or feeding me, for that matter. If I don't hold any significance for you as a person . . .'

'I came to find out what you want for breakfast.'

'Bugger breakfast! I want to get out of here.'

'You left the fried egg and sausage yesterday. Kipper suit you better?'

Louise brandished an arm in despair. 'Just go away.'

He made crabwise for the door. 'A pair of kippers. Out of the freezer, but you can't expect miracles. And you'll want to keep your strength up.'

At eleven by her watch, Louise heard the sound of a car being driven away.

The wind and the downpour seemed to have eased. Inside the room it felt warmer, as if the heating had been turned up. On a tray by the bed, a kipper lay partially dismantled over a thick china plate. Her stomach felt abused. Tension, fear, lack of exercise were conspiring to give her an insistent sick headache: excessive tea-consumption had furred her tongue. She needed fresh air, a proper diet. She needed release. Weeping a little, soundlessly into the pillow, she flogged her weary brain into new channels.

At eleven-twenty she pushed herself off the bed and went into the bathroom. Running the tap experimentally, she found the water steaming. Until now it had been no more than tepid. Thankfully she took a bath, tempted to stay immersed for an hour but forcing herself out after ten minutes, towelling herself gently but thoroughly, putting such unattainables as talc and body lotion out of her mind. With the help of the stained mirror above the washbasin she paid some attention to her hair, combing and arranging it about her face and into her neck in the style that Sally had once told her was flattering. She applied some lipstick. Instead of dressing, she merely wrapped herself in her coat and left it loose at the neck.

Returning to the bedside table, she scraped the kipper remnants on to the tray and placed the empty plate face-down upon the carpet. With the electric kettle in her right hand, she knelt and delivered a light blow to the patterned china.

No result. Harder. The impact was absorbed by the foam underlay. Picking up the plate, she took it to the bathroom and slid it into the washbasin. Taking aim, she let fly once more.

The plate disintegrated. Pieces flew about the room, into the bath. Collecting them carefully, she returned to the main room and deposited them on the tray. Most of the fragments were small. Several were finger-sized, and two or three were about five inches in length. Selecting one of these that tapered to a point, Louise secreted it under the pillow and left the residual pieces where they were, carelessly mingled with the kipper remnants. After a final glance she slipped beneath the bedclothes and lay face upwards, her shoulders uncovered except for the coat, shivering uncontrollably for a while despite the room temperature. Presently she regained command of herself, her breathing, her thoughts.

At ten minutes to one there was a rap at the door. 'Ready for lunch?'

'I'm in bed. You can come in.'

The door rattled, shot open. On the landing, Scott stood with his padded broom handle at the ready: seeing her lying on the far side of the room, he advanced and closed the door behind him, locking it from inside, pocketing the key. He came forward, eyed the tray.

'Been chucking the crockery around?'

'Yes, I'm sorry. I had a slight accident.'

For some reason he looked a shade anxious. 'Cut yourself?'

'No, nothing like that. I just dropped the kettle on it.'

'Oh yeah—I was forgetting.' He fingered the plaster at his hairline. 'It's other people you like knocking around.'

'Only when I'm pushed to it. I've nothing against you, as a person.' Sitting up, she took no action to prevent the coat's collar from sagging a little. She saw his eyes dart. 'Actually,' she went on guilelessly, 'I've been lying here thinking I should apologize to you. I don't approve of violence. It wasn't justified.'

'Taken your time, haven't you, getting round to it?'

'Well, I've not been thinking too straight. Would you, in my position?'

'Couldn't tell you.' A swallowing action disturbed his Adam's apple. 'Want anything to eat?'

'What I'd like is some company.'

'Sorry, lady. Agin the rules.'

Louise gave a sigh. 'There can't be much to keep you downstairs. It get so tedious up here. If I'm left to myself much longer, I'll go insane.'

'You won't. You're not the type.'

'How do you know what type I am?'

'Heard him talking about you.'

'Him? Jackson?'

Scott released a short bark. 'That's it . . . Jackson.'

'Not his real name, I suppose. Who is he? Are you a mate of his, or just helping out?'

'You're asking too many questions. I'm just here to take a lunch order. What d'you fancy? There's beefburgers or there's fish fingers. The burgers—'

'I don't like the sound of either. There's only one thing I'd like, just now.'

'Yeah, you said.' Scott moistened his thin lips. 'Look, lady, I'd like to oblige but I've got orders, okay? I can't stop. Fish fingers?'

From her sitting position against the pillow, Louise gave him a lateral survey in company with a curled lip. 'Driven off, hasn't he? The mythical Jackson. How long will he be away?'

'He'll be back by four.'

'That's three hours. What are you afraid of?'

'I ain't afraid of nothing.'

'So why the excuses?'

'Listen, I told you. I've got—'

'Don't tell me. You've had your orders. Lucky old you. Such a handy let-out.' Pouting, Louise slid down into a semi-recumbent posture, allowing one side of the coat collar to flap open. Clasping it absently, she steered it some of the way back. 'Run along, then, and dish up your fish fingers and frozen peas. You'll make somebody a grand little wife, one of these years.'

Scott stood looking down at her, his features vacant. Presently he returned slowly to the door, took out the key, weighed it in his palm. From the bed, Louise reached out for a copy of *Woman's Weekly* that lay on the floor, further disarranging her coat with the movement. This time she made no effort to replace it as she settled back, opening the magazine to the centrefold, studying it fixedly.

When he came back, she failed to notice him. He stationed himself at the foot of the bed, his eyes busy. Louise read on. Scott let out a cough.

'I could stay half an hour. Only you'd have to go without your lunch.'

She looked indifferently over the top of the page. 'Still here? I thought you were crouched over a hot cooker. What was that?'

'I said, I can stop on for a bit.' His voice was hoarse. 'But I can't do a meal an' all.'

'I wouldn't want you to tire yourself.' She allowed the magazine to slide off the coverlet. 'Well.' She gazed at him brightly. 'If we've only a short while, let's not waste any of it. Why not sit down, make yourself comfortable?'

She patted the bed-edge. Scott shuffled along and sat gingerly, depressing the mattress. His lean, drawn face seemed inadequate to house the emotions of which he was plainly a victim. Putting out an arm, Louise ran her fingers teasingly down his badly-shaven jowl and on to his neck, feeling a muscle twitch.

'You're all tensed-up,' she chided, shrugging the coat clear of her right shoulder. 'No need for that. In a little while you'll be feeling much better . . . we both shall. Who wants fish fingers anyway? Cruelty to cod, that's what it is.'

Scott's taut mouth stretched in something adjacent to a grin. '*That's* right,' she crooned, falling back and looking up at him assessingly. 'You know, you've a good smile. Nice teeth. You could have anyone you chose. Ever thought about that?'

With a gulp, Scott began peeling off his jacket. Lending a helpful hand, Louise completed the process of shaking her own coat down to waist level and, with rising nausea, saw his eyes develop a bulge. His shirt smelt musty. Quickly, before she was ill. 'Oh, my dear. Quite eager, weren't you, after all? And here was I, thinking you were being—'

Half the breath exploded from her lungs as he fell upon her. With shock and alarm, she realized that she had miscalculated. The spring had been tightened: now that it was uncoiling, nothing could stem its effect. Her limbs were pinned. The thin lips slobbered over her. Any second now, she would throw up. 'You're hurting . . .'

Briefly the pressure eased as he switched position, swarming further on to the mattress before grappling with her again. It gave her a precious second. Her right hand slid backwards, groped beneath the pillow. For a heart-stopping moment her fingers found nothing; then, as Scott returned to the charge, they made contact. Grasping the china segment firmly, she eased her arm clear, brought it up and around behind his back.

He was making mumbling noises into her left ear. Raising the arm as high as she dared, she steadied the fragment, point downwards, and brought it down hard.

CHAPTER 11

Kevin was first to emerge from the school gates, cap awry, shoulder-bag unstrapped, knees purpled by the breeze. Spotting Fletcher in the usual place, he slowed, bade farewell to a classmate, sauntered up to the car and clambered on to the front passenger seat.

'Terri's coming,' he informed his father. 'She had to stay behind.'

'Why's that?'

'She didn't answer when Miss Pritchard spoke to her at dinner-time.'

'Will she be long?'

'Only a few minutes.' Hauling a video magazine from

his bag, Kevin examined an inside page with concentration.

Fletcher sat with consternation gnawing at his vitals. To his relief, Terri on emergence looked her normal self, although she was even less communicative than her brother. Miss Pritchard, it seemed, had made her sit upright in a chair for two minutes, by herself, but hadn't grumbled at her. No, Terri didn't dislike Miss Pritchard. Yes, she would be good in future, answer when spoken to. In putting the questions, Fletcher felt that he was being demanding, unreasonable: patiently as she dealt with them, Terri conveyed the impression that her presence was required elsewhere and she really shouldn't be detained. When he desisted, she fell silent, staring out of the car window at the scurrying peak-hour traffic. Kevin remained apparently engrossed by video technology. Worried about the pair of them, Fletcher drove badly.

As they walked down the driveway, Eva opened the front door to them. 'Spotted you arrive,' she announced. 'Everyone ready for a meal?'

The children went silently past her into the hallway. Eva turned to their father with a smile. 'Bruising day? You look done up.' Closing the door, she planted a kiss on his cheek.

'A little ragged at the edges,' he said quietly. 'Don't expect conversation just yet.' Dumping his coat on the chair, he went on into the living-room, sat down, turned his attention to his shoelaces. From the doorway, Eva observed him.

'When you feel like it, I'll fix us a drink.' She withdrew to the kitchen.

The children reappeared, divested of outer garments, to watch forty minutes of *Scrapbook*. The programme's tub-thumping exuberance gave Fletcher the sensation that he was being struck continually about the head with cement-filled coloured balloons, but it plugged the gap until supper. Afterwards, there was a vintage Buster Keaton comedy to perform a similar function while Eva cleared away. Midway through the film, Fletcher rose stealthily and left the room to make a phone call.

After ringing off, he stood irresolute for a moment before entering the kitchen. Eva was scouring the residue of fried liver from a pan. Her stance was pensive. At Fletcher's appearance she glanced around. 'Any news from Dawson, or Inspector Cummings?'

'No official news from anywhere.' He placed faint stress on the second word. Leaning against the refrigerator, he watched her movements. She brought them to a halt.

'Unofficial?'

'Possibly.'

'What's the matter?' she asked, after an interval.

He said nothing. Removing the pan from the sink, she placed it on the drainer, turned fully, dried her fingers on a length of paper towelling, dropped it into the bin. 'Come on, love. I know when I'm being wordlessly quizzed. Let's have it.'

'I saw Ferrari today,' he said abruptly.

'I thought you'd finished with him. What did he have to say?'

'Quite a lot.'

Eva waited. 'Well?'

Fletcher glanced at the door. 'I was going to let it ride until they were in bed, but . . . He told me about the man in the car.'

'The Mercedes?'

'The other one—the Sierra. He's called Bradley and a few alternative names, and he's a minor crook.'

Eva frowned. 'So?'

'Ferrari's been making some inquiries about him. His contacts and associates.'

'And?'

'It seems that just lately Bradley's been having quite a

bit to do with a car dealer in this area . . . a guy by the name of Deedes. Jock Deedes. He runs a firm called Square Deal Motors, with premises in Abingmore. Heard of them?'

Eva shook her head, not in denial. 'I don't see where this gets us. Ferrari's just tossing you a few scraps to get the assignment back. You're not taking any notice of what he says?'

Fletcher disregarded the query. 'The reason I thought you might know of the firm,' he said, 'is that Deedes happens to be your maiden surname. That's right, isn't it? You mentioned it once. Seems coincidental. It's not that common a name around here.'

Eva stood in an attitude of consideration, her head tilted to one side. 'Jock Deedes,' she said at last, 'is my brother, that's perfectly true. And he's been in touch with some lag called Bradley? Hardly surprising. He's a motor dealer. People in his trade are apt to bump up against all sorts. This Bradley specimen—maybe he was after a particular make of car, and my brother . . .'

'This was no trade matter. From what Ferrari could glean, Bradley and your brother Jock were in constant touch over a period of days a couple of weeks back—at the car showrooms and in a local pub—but it wasn't about a car. If it had been, one of the salesmen or a mechanic would have known about it.'

'All right,' Eva said reasonably. 'It wasn't to do with a sale. Perhaps Jock has a roofing problem at his premises. Wanted a cut-price quotation, something like that.'

Fletcher gave her a hard look. 'How did you know Bradley's in the roofing business?'

'He sounds the type who might be.' She gestured. 'There are dozens of cowboy contractors who—'

'Don't fence with me, Eva. That I can't take. You know Bradley, don't you?'

Picking up a pan, she gave it a wipe with a cloth,

returned it to its rack, began swishing hot water around the sink. 'I might know *of* him,' she said presently. 'Jock mentions a lot of people. Now that I think of it, he was trying to set up a home servicing scheme recently, and he was on the look-out for a qualified man. Could that have been Bradley?'

'There's something else Ferrari found out.'

Displaying no curiosity, Eva went on sluicing the stainless steel. Fletcher walked across, gripped her by an elbow. 'A Mercedes,' he said evenly, 'came into your brother's showroom back in January.'

'What of it?'

'After it had been serviced and resprayed, it stood around for a while and then—according to one of the mechanics, who was a blabbermouth after a couple of pints—it was driven off by your brother and hasn't been seen since. There's no record of a sale. It just seemed to vanish.'

'You're hurting my arm. What's Ferrari trying to prove?'

'He's trying to establish a few probabilities, that's all. One of them is that your brother Jock still has the use of the Mercedes. Also, if he wanted to change the number plates for reasons of his own, he's in a good position to do so.'

'I don't know what you're suggesting. What would Jock want with a car like that?'

'Good question. According to Ferrari's helpful mechanic, your brother continues to run a Datsun hatchback which he keeps in the single garage of his town house in Abingmore. If he wanted to run a second car, you'd think he'd keep it at the showrooms—but there's been no sign of it. Another fact that emerged . . .'

'Telephone,' Eva said suddenly.

Releasing her, Fletcher strode out of the kitchen to answer the call. A voice he didn't recognize said, 'Mrs

Maynard there? Can I talk to her?'

'She is here,' Fletcher replied on a note of reserve. 'Who wants her?'

'Tell her it's Jock. Could you make it a bit snappy? It's urgent.'

Fletcher returned to the kitchen. 'Your brother, wanting to talk to you. Sounds in a flap.'

Without comment, Eva went out. Turning off a ring of the cooker which had been left aglow, Fletcher dampened a sponge and set about removing greasespots from the oven door. He was going on to eliminate fingermarks from cupboard handles when Eva reappeared, closing the door softly behind her and standing against it. She looked a little pale.

Moving across, he confronted her. She spoke in an undertone. 'Pay attention, love. You'll have to know. Jock's been holding Louise since she went off. He's doing it for us.'

Fletcher stood rigid, staring at her. '*Holding?* What's that supposed to mean?'

Eva made a small restive movement. 'Keeping her away. Setting things up.'

'For Christ's sake. Whose mad idea was that?'

'It sort of evolved between us. Jock was anxious to do something, for my sake. So when you told me that Louise had advertised, I suggested Mr Rosenberg, and Jock did the rest.'

'Just who the hell *is* Rosenberg?'

'He's a salesman. Name of Derek Crofts. He works at the showrooms, and Jock has some kind of a hold over him—some shady deal he knows about. So he was able to talk him into acting the part of Rosenberg. Crofts was ideal for the purpose. He has a very smooth manner and a way with the ladies, and he knows how to fling money around. He was perfect.'

'Eva, let me be absolutely sure about what you're

saying. You and your brother, between you, hatched a family plot to deprive my children of their mother?'

'For *us*,' she insisted. 'It was the only way. Your method was futile. Ferrari was collecting no evidence to speak of against Louise, was he? Something had to be done.'

'Kidnap?'

'Not kidnap—detention. It was such a marvellous opportunity, don't you see? When you mentioned Louise's ad in the *Gleaner*, it was as if you'd purposely opened a door.'

'I never dreamt . . . How did you go about it?'

Eva shrugged. 'Simply typed a letter in reply, as from "Mr Rosenberg", giving my home phone number. Next day I had a call from Louise . . . you were right, the ad was hers and she'd no false modesty in chasing up answers. I put on a fake accent, pretended to be a secretary, and things developed from there. Temporary detention—that's all it was. Can't you see that?'

'With what object? To send her and the kids off their rockers?'

'Don't be absurd.' Eva seized his hand. 'Love, it's perfectly simple. Look at it from the viewpoint of an outsider. Louise makes contact with "Mr Rosenberg", falls under his spell, goes off with him, leaves the kids uncared for. When she gets back, a week or so later, what's the position? She's the woman who abandoned her family, the woman who—'

'All she has to do is say what really happened.'

'Who's going to believe her?'

'She can prove . . .' Fletcher paused.

'She made no secret of the liaison. It all went on in full public view. She left of her own free will.'

'Yes—thinking she was going to be back in a few hours.'

'Who's to know that? Besotted women have been known to change their minds, even though they may have left hurried notes for their children. In Louise's case, "Mr Rosenberg" was just too much for her. That's the clear inference, and no amount of details will help her much when it comes to a new court hearing over custody.'

Fletcher paced away to the cooker and back. 'You're forgetting something. This phoney Rosenberg character—Crofts—he'll have to give evidence that she was with him somewhere: his own home, presumably, if that's where she's being kept.'

'It's all fixed. He's agreed to do that.'

'But then his true identity will have to come out. How does he explain the "Rosenberg" set-up?'

'Easy. He was shy about answering a personal ad, so he did it under an assumed name. That must happen quite a lot.'

'You're missing the point. When it becomes known that he's Derek Crofts and that he works for Jock Deedes, the connection with you might be spotlighted. That could be a dead giveaway.'

Eva shook a confident head. 'It's not too likely. Nobody in the district would know that I'm Jock's sister. We've kept in touch by phone, but we'd not met physically for a couple of years until we got together to work out details of this scheme, and then we each drove to a spot in Abingmore Forest and talked out of sight of anybody. My dear, it's foolproof. Why should anyone connect us?'

Fletcher chewed his lower lip. 'A lot depends on where Louise has actually been kept. According to Ferrari—'

Eva's uplifted hand cut him off. Putting a finger to her lips, she turned and opened the kitchen door to admit a surge of finale-style music and reveal the indecisive figure of Kevin in the living-room doorway. 'Is the film over?' she asked.

The boy nodded. 'Can we have some cocoa?'

'If you say please. I'll bring it to you, and some biscuits. How was Buster Keaton?'

'All right.'

'What's on now?'

'Football.' He went back inside and closed the door. Eva stood looking at it for a moment before returning to the kitchen to face Fletcher once more. He was standing motionless by the table, staring down at it. She approached him.

'What a relief when this is over. Poor kids. They can't understand what's hit them.'

'There was no need,' he said, low-voiced, 'for anything to hit them. I can't collect my thoughts . . . What was I saying? Ferrari, that's it. He unearthed another fact about your brother Jock. It seems he owns an isolated farmhouse about thirty miles east of here, between Wallingford and Oxford. He bought it as an investment three years ago and it's stood unoccupied ever since. He rents out a few fields to a local cattleman, but most of the farmland is unworked.'

Fletcher paused. No repudiation came from Eva. Quietly he added, 'Is that where he's keeping Louise?'

After a moment's hesitation she nodded. 'It's completely safe. Nobody within a mile, apart from the cattleman. He lives in a shack on the edge of the estate and takes no notice of anything except his cows.'

Fletcher pondered for a while, before glancing up from the table. 'This Steve Bradley. Or Scott, whatever. He's part of your abduction squad—right? But he seemed to be involved much earlier. Ferrari spotted him parked outside the school some while before Louise's ad appeared and gave you this crazy idea. What was he doing there at that time?'

'Just sizing things up,' Eva said calmly. 'As you know, I never expected Ferrari to produce much. So I contacted Jock, who roped in Steve—he's worked for him before. Steve started to keep tabs on the people concerned, in the hope of concocting some workable plan. Then he was chased through Bancester by some car—Ferrari's, I assume—so he had to lay off. Soon after that, Louise's ad was published. Problem solved. That's when we brought in Derek Crofts.'

'Why wait until now,' Fletcher demanded, 'to tell me all this?'

'But for Ferrari, you needn't have known at all. We thought it was better that you shouldn't. We knew there'd be questions. As long as you were in the dark, anything you said was going to sound convincing. And it worked, didn't it?'

'Did it?' He shook his head, like a dog trying to rid himself of a drenching. 'So why the change of policy now? Is it over? Is Louise on her way back?'

Stretching past him, Eva tugged open a cupboard door and took down a tin of cocoa powder. She began forcing off the lid. She said, 'There's been a development.'

CHAPTER 12

At the fork, on Eva's less than categorical instructions, Fletcher steered to the right, followed a half-mile stretch of undulating lane to a junction with a main road, where after more hesitancy she told him to go left.

After a few hundred yards, a selection of place-names on a sign blazed in their headlamps, and Eva relaxed slightly inside her seat-harness. 'I think we're on our way.'

Fletcher drove robot-like, his mind elsewhere. His long-distance glasses kept steaming up. He passed them to Eva to wipe. 'We're making slow time,' he muttered distractedly. 'What time did Sally say she must get back to her mother?'

'Ten, or soon after. We'll do it. Anyhow her mother

won't peg out, will she, for the sake of an extra twenty minutes?'

'How would I know? She may need injections or something. Eva . . .'

'Yes, love?'

'What's this all about? Why does Jock need us there? Is Louise . . . ?'

'She's okay.'

'Then why the sudden panic? If the idea was to keep her until—'

'You're asking me things I don't know. We'll find out, soon enough.'

'This wasn't the original plan, was it? You were just going to let her turn up again. What's happened to alter that?'

'Let's wait and see.' Eva's hands were balled on her lap; otherwise she seemed composed. She added, 'It's probably nothing. Jock's liable to get worked up, for no reason.'

'Sounds just the dependable type we need,' Fletcher said bitingly. 'What possessed you to rope him in?'

'He had the car,' she pointed out, 'and the contacts. Plus the hideout, which was vital. As for motivation . . .'

'Brotherly affection, I suppose.'

'We've always been close, that's true. Even when we've not met up, like in the past year or two, we've stayed in touch. He'd do anything for me. And besides, he's suffered himself, the same as you.'

'The custody struggle over his daughter? After that, I'd have thought he wouldn't want any more fights on his hands.'

'Bear right here at the roundabout.' When the switch of direction was accomplished, Eva went on dreamily, 'In his own way, Jock's a bit of a crusader. Feels very strongly now about divorce settlements, paternal rights . . . all that. It's the reason I didn't hesitate. I knew he'd want to see justice done, even if I hadn't been his sister.'

'You pitched him the full story, I take it?'

'Naturally. He had to know the background.'

'Since he got his daughter back,' said Fletcher, half a mile on, 'Jock's looked after her alone, is that it? No other female in his life?'

'Not likely. He's had an overdose.'

'The way it sounds, he could be pathologically biased against the female parent-figure. You're quite sure he hasn't done Louise some harm?'

'Jock would never do anything of the sort. Stop imagining things.' In the glare from an oncoming vehicle, she turned in her seat to peer at him. 'Supposing he had—why should you care? What has Louise done for you, in heaven's name, to deserve sympathy?'

The entrance to a shallow lay-by loomed ahead. Turning into it with wrenching suddenness, Fletcher steered a weaving course to a standstill at the farther end before yanking up the handbrake. Another car passed at speed, its engine-note dying in the distance, leaving them in darkness and solitude. Eva remained still. Turning slightly towards her, Fletcher spoke on a metronomic beat.

'Now listen. What went on between my ex-wife and myself is neither here nor there. I've no overwhelming reason to feel regard for her. You might say I've good cause to resent her existence, as she probably does mine. But one thing I hope I'm not, and that's vindictive. You should know that by now. I want this thing settled in an orderly way: not by violence. Physical abuse of anyone, least of all a woman, is something I could never tolerate. Is that clear?'

'Crystal.' Eva lifted both arms, let them fall back. 'I'm with you, love, all the way. No need to get all hot and bothered.'

'It's what you said, about not caring . . .'

'I shouldn't have said that. It's not what I meant. I just . . .' She paused. 'Perhaps it was my way of asking how you still feel about *me*.'

Fletcher tapped the wheel. 'Why should you feel you need to ask?'

'That's what I'm wondering.'

For a few moments neither of them spoke. Something rustled in the hedge alongside them; seconds later, as though in response to the signal, a heavy goods vehicle thundered past, its slipstream rocking the car. Silence crawled back. Reaching for the ignition key, Fletcher fired the engine, kept it idling as he gazed over the wheel.

He said, 'You came to my aid at a critical time. You've looked after my family when they needed someone. I'll always be grateful for that.'

'Grateful.'

She repeated the word neither as question nor comment, articulating each syllable as if chewing cyanide. Ill at ease, he let in the clutch and nosed back on to the road, picking up speed as his mirror showed him darkness behind. After a mile he spoke again.

'I'm not clear just now, Eva, about my feelings. The situation's too confused. Let it ride for the moment.'

A cattle-grid clattered under the wheels. As the gateposts ghosted by, a burst of light dazzled him, prompting him to stamp on the footbrake. The car shuddered to a halt.

'Switch off main beam,' advised Eva. 'He'll want to check that it's us.'

Fletcher flicked the control. For an instant they remained floodlit, like a yacht in harbour; then the twin beams ahead of them were dipped, allowing them gradually to discern the outline of a car parked with its tail to the doors of an outhouse. Feet began audibly crossing the yard. Eva shaded her eyes.

'It's Jock. He's coming over.'

Silhouetted against the glare, the figure that approached had a stooped look to it, as of someone trying to come to terms with a sudden burden slung around the neck. It came direct to the passenger window, which Eva had wound down.

'For God's sake, Sis. You took your time.'

'It's a thirty-mile drive, and we had to get a child-minder first.' She placed a soothing hand on his wrist. 'We've arrived. What's the problem?'

Ducking his head, her brother peered through at Fletcher. 'This him?'

'Colin, I'd like you to meet Jock. He's the only—'

'Save it, Sis. We've things to discuss. Take the car through to the inner yard, will you? Douse the lights, then come over to the house. Don't hang about.'

'Likely to sit admiring the view, aren't we?' Concern showed through Eva's irony. Jock was already striding back to his own car. 'Do as he says,' she instructed Fletcher, examining the dim mass of the farmhouse. 'Once we're inside, I can get some sense out of him.'

Refraining from comment, Fletcher nudged the car through the second entrance and bounced across flagstones to a corner of the walled enclosure, where he switched everything off. His heart had begun to pump. Climbing out, he held the door for Eva, then followed her to a door of the house which Jock, having extinguished his headlamps, had reached ahead of them and was holding open.

In the low-power light from the hall ceiling, Fletcher was able to make out his features. They were an odd mix of cragginess and fragility, adding up to a landscape which, on the face of it, might by turn look acceptable or bleak, depending upon weather conditions. The present climate, in Fletcher's judgement, was far from temperate. Jock's mottled-pink facial skin was stretched across his cheekbones as though it had been stitched back: his sandy hair was in disarray. Barely waiting to get inside, Fletcher confronted him nose to nose.

'Has anything happened to her? Is she hurt?'

'It's not Louise.' Stepping between them, Eva propelled them apart. 'It's Bradley—right, Jock? You said something had cropped up. What is it? Has his past caught up with him, or something?'

Jock aimed a foot at the door, slamming it shut. 'Steve's had it.'

She stared at him uncomprehendingly for a moment. 'Opted out, you mean? Pushed off?'

'No, that's not what I mean.' He avoided her gaze. 'She did for him. It happened while I was away. There was nothing I could do. Honestly, Sis. Everything was going to plan. I just don't know what got into Steve. He must have lost his marbles.'

Stepping forward, Eva shook him by the lapels. 'Jock, will you make sense? You're not saying they've *both* gone off—together?'

'I'm saying Steve's dead.'

Eva stood examining him with an air of curiosity, as if he had let slip an item of information that could not be related to the matter in hand. A dreamlike sensation overtook Fletcher. Presently he would awake; this improbable scene would dissolve, like mist in summer's heat. In the meantime he was looking on, a bystander with nothing to contribute. Passively he watched Eva take her brother's arm, steer him away, kick open a door at the rear end of the hall and disappear with him inside. Fletcher felt like the unwanted guest awaiting the offer of a hot wash. A cowhide chair stood against a wall near by. Wobbling across to it, he sat heavily.

I'm hallucinating, he thought. Eva has no brother called Jock. Nobody exists by the name of Steve Bradley: nobody is dead. He waited dully for something normal to occur. The hall seemed to become colder.

Emerging from the rear door, Eva tip-tapped over the tiled floor, wearing an expression like an asbestos mask, flameproof, emotion-free. Crouching before him, she rested a hand on each of his knees.

'It's true, apparently. Louise stabbed him. We've got decisions to make.'

Fletcher gazed at her. 'Such as what?' he heard himself ask.

She gave an impatient twitch of the shoulders. 'The best way, of course, to exploit the situation. Jock's useless. He's gone to pieces. We'll have to take over.'

'Has he notified the police?'

'We need time to work something out. There's a drink, if you want one.'

'Work something out,' Fletcher repeated mechanically. 'I don't follow.'

'Don't be *stupid*.' Seeing him recoil, she moderated her tone. 'Love, we have to step carefully. In one sense it's a disaster, but there might be something . . . Let's think about it.'

'What the hell are you on about, Eva? How was Bradley killed?'

'Louise used a piece of broken china. He's lying upstairs.'

'And where is she?'

'In a storeroom at the back. Jock arrived back just in time to grab her as she was leaving the house.'

Fletcher pressed his eyelids with thumb and forefinger. 'What time did it happen?'

'Early afternoon, apparently. Jock had gone into Wallingford to buy a few things: he got back here about one-thirty. Louise rushed out as he was unloading the car. She was hysterical. Blood all over her. He thought she'd tried to commit suicide. He had to be . . . quite firm with her to get her back inside. Then he locked her in the storeroom while he went to look for Steve. He found him on Louise's bed in the attic. He's still there.'

' "Quite firm". What does that mean?'

'We haven't gone into detail,' Eva said precisely. 'Don't worry about it. Jock wouldn't do more than was necessary.'

'You said he's apt to lose his head. How can you know what he might have done?'

'I do know what Louise did to Steve. That wasn't in the book, so we may have to rewrite a chapter. There's no reason—'

'Book? Chapter? For Christ's sake, Eva. You talk like an East End mobster. All right, so Louise stabbed this confederate of yours—can you blame her? Held captive, wasn't she? Not knowing what was happening, frantic about her children. Of course she reacted. Now, you seem to be suggesting she's committed a culpable offence and we ought to capitalize on it somehow. What's got into you?'

'In the first place,' Eva said steadily, after a brief delay, 'don't get the idea I'm shedding tears of blood for Steve Bradley. He was no particular buddy of mine. In the second place, since when was wilful killing *not* an offence? Louise was in no danger. Her life wasn't threatened. She'd only to—'

'Did she know that?'

'What?'

'She knew she was going to get out alive? Somebody told her?'

'Look, we've a problem on our hands. Sitting here arguing about it isn't going to help. Practical suggestions—they're what's needed. Do you have one?'

Rising violently from the chair, Fletcher sent her spinning backwards against the opposite wall. 'I've made my suggestion. Call the police. It should have been done hours ago. Where's the phone?'

'Colin.' There was a rasping edge to Eva's voice. 'It's

not on, do you hear? Not yet. Not until everything's worked out.'

He stood looking at her. 'You mean, until you and that half-baked brother of yours have devised some way of shifting the responsibility? Is that it?'

'Shifting? I don't see the need. Louise did it, all right. No dispute about that.'

'You know damn well what I'm driving at. It's a question of whether what she did was justifiable, and by God, there can't be much dispute about that, either. Show me the telephone. I'm getting the authorities along here right now, and you're going to explain the whole thing to them. This lunacy has gone far enough.'

Her eyes had acquired a brilliance that he had not seen in them before. Spine to the wall, she remained motionless, silent. Turning, he strode towards the rear door, halted, came back. 'I want to see Louise. Get Jock to take me along.'

'You're behaving like a fool. Don't you see what a chance we've been handed? We set out, didn't we, to blacken Louise's character as a parent? Now we're in a position to have her put away for years. Isn't that something worth fighting for? Don't pass it up, Colin love.'

Moving clear of the wall, she advanced with outstretched arms, putting Fletcher hideously in mind of a somnambulant Lady Macbeth. 'I know this has come as a shock to you. We've just got to keep our nerve. If we all—'

He eluded her reach. 'Have a word with your brother. I want him to take me to Louise: after that, I want a call made to the police. Do I make myself absolutely clear?'

Eva froze. 'You don't seem to understand what I've been saying. All right. Have it your way. You'll wish you'd listened to me.' Her tone was that of a sorrowful mother rebuking a fractious teenager. 'Come through,' she added, sweeping past him.

Jock was straddling an arm of a shabby sofa on the upper portion of a split-level living-room, a low-ceilinged area connected to the lower section by three ornamental wrought-iron steps. Modern radiators gave out heat to excess. In Jock's right hand nestled a quarter-full whisky glass. There was no sign of a bottle. Walking across to him, Eva said something partly under her breath. Jock glanced up.

'Where's the sense in that?' His gaze roamed over Fletcher with a kind of anguished apathy. Eva spread her hands.

'It's what he wants. Try talking him out of it.'

Her brother came groggily to his feet. 'Why the cops?' he demanded. 'Steve won't be missed. If he didn't show up for six months, nobody'd be the wiser.'

'So what are you worried about?' asked Fletcher.

'You're doing the worrying.' With an unconvincing display of indifference, Jock downed the last of his drink before dumping the glass on a shelf above a radiator.

'One of us has to do something. You called us here. That seems to indicate you don't feel up to handling things.' Fletcher nodded at the whisky glass. 'I doubt if that'll help much.'

'He's just had the one,' Eva interposed. 'He needed it to steady up.'

'That I can believe.'

'Weighty with his opinions, isn't he?' Jock nodded in Fletcher's direction. 'Thought you said he was easygoing.'

'Colin's under stress . . . we all are. Which is one reason I think we should hold our horses. Not blab it all out to the police, handing them the entire picture before we—'

'The longer we leave it,' said Fletcher, 'the worse it'll be, in the end. You can't cover up a sudden death.'

'Who said anything about covering it up?'

'A moment ago, you seemed to be hinting at any number of possibilities.'

Eva consulted her brother, who shrugged. 'What's all the hassle?" he asked. 'There's been an accident—a fatality. If we can't manipulate things so that—'

'Pipe down, Jock.' She motioned him into silence. 'Colin's not having anything of that sort, and he's right. Killing Steve was just a reflex action on Louise's part. If we set out to pin the total blame on her, how do we explain it all to the police? Bound to ask questions, aren't they? We can't expect them to swallow our version and ignore hers.'

'They don't have to swallow it.' An element of slyness had crept into her brother's voice. 'Not in one lump. We can feed it to them, selectively.'

'How do you mean?'

'Think about it. What was it the law was going to be asked to believe? That the Fletcher woman came here of her own accord with "Mr Rosenberg"—right? So, fine, that's the way the story stays. One small difference, though.'

'What's that?'

'The bit concerning Steve. He came along with "Rosenberg" to cook the meals and generally look after the pair of them, okay? Near enough the truth. The embroidered touch is, Steve then got ideas of his own about Louise.'

'Go on,' Eva said thoughtfully.

'What is there to add?' Jock looked triumphantly from his sister to Fletcher. ' "Rosenberg" had to go out for a few hours. While he was gone, Steve tried to take advantage, Louise fought him off with a broken plate . . . and zap! No blame attached. Justifiable self-defence. What d'you say?'

Eva was frowning. 'There's still the link with you and me. It's your farmhouse. You'd have to account for—'

'Sis, it makes no difference. The original story stands. "Rosenberg" is a mate of mine. I loaned him the farmhouse so he could have it away with his new bird . . . that was the extent of my involvement. Simple.'

'And where's "Rosenberg" now?'

'Taken fright. Scarpered. No problem there. Derek's got itchy feet; he was leaving anyway. I'll tell him to take off for London, keep there out of sight. He can take the Merc with him. Neat, huh?'

'All quite tidy,' Eva said slowly. 'From our viewpoint, that is. How do we get Louise to obligingly back up that version of events?'

Her brother had regained poise. His voice sounded assured. 'We've still got her over a barrel. Unless she cooperates, those kids of hers will always be at risk. That'll do it. You should see her eyes when they're brought into the conversation. She won't take chances.'

'She could tell the police. Ask for protection.'

'She knows they can't watch 'em indefinitely. Makes more sense for her to go along with us, avoid the uncertainty. Besides . . .'

'Besides what?'

'You've got to remember, Louise is one very confused and frightened lady. She's killed a man. Right now, she's rocky about her legal position. She's in shock. If we advise her, she'll listen. Count on it.'

Fletcher had been following the exchange with mounting incredulity. Unable to contain himself, he now stepped forward, gripped Jock by the left arm, whirled him around, sent him staggering down the wrought-iron steps to the lower level where he recovered balance by clutching the edge of a heavy oak table.

'You have to be insane,' Fletcher said furiously. 'A story like that—it would explode around your ears. Even assuming you could con Louise into supporting it, any half-wit of a country copper could blast it full of holes in five seconds. Stop trying to fool yourselves.'

'It's only one option.' Rubbing his arm, Jock planted

himself on the table, transmitting a wary glance to his sister over the handrail. 'We've others to choose from. I tell you, Steve won't be missed. We can dump him, carry on as if nothing had happened. Nobody knows he's been here. Or we can—'

'Cut it out, do you hear? Shut him up, Eva. I've had enough. Louise is the person I want to speak to, not drivelling maniacs. Give me the key to the storeroom.'

'Do as he says, Jock.'

Eva's brother looked mutinous. Then he sagged. 'You want to pack it in without a struggle? Up to you. We were just trying to help.'

From a back pocket of his cord trousers he produced a Yale key, tossed it up the miniature staircase to Fletcher, who caught it at the second attempt. Jock scratched his jaw. 'Sis—you reckon this calls for a chaser? Seems I shan't be needing a clear head, after all.'

'Suit yourself. Where do you keep the phone? If Colin's going down to the storeroom, I'll be making the call.'

'At last you're talking sense.' Fletcher breathed in. His chest felt constricted, as if he had been running hard. 'Tell them to get along here as soon as they possibly can.' He glanced back at Jock. 'Do we need an ambulance, as well? What shape is Louise in?'

'Fit as a flea,' scoffed the motor-dealer.

'How do I get to the storeroom?'

'Through the kitchen, door on the left, down the steps, door facing you at the bottom. Mind how you go.'

Ignoring the sneer, Fletcher said stonily to Eva, 'Put that call through, will you? Enough time's been wasted.'

Strip lighting in the kitchen exposed it as a sizeable, pink-painted room, well equipped, reasonably clean, devoid of any humanizing quality. A heavy board door in the far left corner was secured by a wooden latch. Beyond it, half a dozen stone steps took him down to the second door, a solid affair of what looked like assembled railway sleepers bonded by metal hoops and hung on hinges that seemed capable of carrying with some comfort the Great Gate of Kiev. On to this formidable barrier had been grafted the brass disc of a Yale lock. The key entered with reluctance. Twisting it several times, Fletcher felt the mechanism give, leaned his weight on the sleepers. The leading edge snagged against the frame: he had to administer a kick before it would swing inwards.

Darkness greeted him. Groping for a switch, he found nothing. Then he spotted one on the wall outside, facing the steps. Flicking it down, he introduced weak light into the storeroom and went through.

After the warmth of the house, the chill of the place prodded him like numbed fingertips. The room was about ten feet square with a concrete floor, brick walls, a plastered ceiling. Part of it was occupied by paper sacks that evidently contained potatoes: to judge from the dust, they had been there a considerable time. There were also some plastic bags of peat fertilizer, a rack of apples sprouting mould, and hanging against one wall a selection of rusty tools plus, on the floor below them, an aluminium wheelbarrow and a power-driven hedge trimmer, corroding rapidly. In the opposite corner, Louise lay curled on her side on a pile of empty plastic sacks. Fletcher crouched beside her.

'It's me. How are you feeling?'

She didn't stir. Inspecting her more closely, he saw that what he had taken for a shadow across her face was in fact a discolouration of the skin, travelling from the left cheekbone up to the temple. 'That bastard up there,' he muttered, 'said you were fine. What happened?'

Eva's brother had been right about one thing. Louise was deep in shock. Under the dim light, Fletcher could see the fixed bulging of her eyes, the shallowness of her breathing. Which was the correct approach? He put out a hand to touch her, retracted it hastily.

'As soon as you feel up to it,' he said on a casual note, 'we'll go back upstairs. I'll fix you a drink. Then we can . . .'

He paused. A trickle of coagulated blood ran from Louise's mouth. Cautiously raising her upper lip, he saw that two of the top teeth were missing. The gum had been severely gashed. Producing his handkerchief, he folded it to a pad and applied it lightly. 'Someone's going to pay for this,' he informed the room. 'I've been misled, but from now on—'

His voice snapped off as Louise's face was extinguished.

For an instance the occurrence failed to register. It was the thud of the door behind him that restored awareness, galvanized him to leap across the floor, scrabble futilely at the railway sleepers while they were still vibrating in the doorframe. There was nothing to grasp. Beating with a fist, he heard the click-click of the lock mechanism, a faint retreat of footsteps. The thump of a more distant door, at greater altitude. After that, the silence.

CHAPTER 13

'Mr Fletcher, please.'

'I'm afraid he's not here.' Sally had expected the call to be from her mother, demanding to know how much longer she was going to be. 'Who's calling?'

'When he gets back, could you tell him Ferrari called?'

'Certainly. I'll ask him to phone back, shall I?'

The voice hesitated. 'If it's inside the next hour or so. Otherwise I'll be in touch with him tomorrow. Sorry you've been troubled.'

'Quite all right. No trouble.'

Hanging up, Sally became aware of being watched. She glanced towards the staircase. A small figure in nightie and dressing-gown was huddled near the newel-post, gazing at her mutely. 'Terri,' she said, on as severe a key as she could touch. 'What are you doing out of bed?'

Approaching the child, she took her by a small, cold hand and towed her towards the living-room door. 'You shouldn't come downstairs just because the phone rings. Come and get warm by the fire before you go back. Like some hot milk?'

'No, thank you.' Terri looked down intently at her fingers.

'Your dad will be home soon. We don't want him to find you down here, do we, when you should be asleep?'

'Kevin was calling out,' said Terri, with jolting irrelevance.

'Kevin was what?'

'He woke me up.'

'No, dear. The telephone woke you.'

'Has Daddy gone to get Mummy?'

'He . . . It's not been fixed yet, when she's . . .' Sally began to flounder. 'She might have to be away,' she amended firmly, 'for a little while longer. So you've both got to keep on behaving yourselves, just as you have been . . . okay? Then we can give her a glowing report. Your dad's very pleased with you, I know.' She held the door invitingly open. 'Coming inside?'

Freeing her hand, Terri turned and trotted along the hall to the stairs. 'I'll go back to bed,' she announced.

'That's a good girl.' Sally watched her helplessly. 'Go to sleep quickly. You'll see Daddy in the morning.'

Subsiding back into the armchair from which she had been eyeing the nine o'clock news, Sally expelled a deep breath and wondered agitatedly whether she had said the right things. It was so difficult to know. Parents, she had heard, quite often found it tricky, and that was when circumstances were normal. An ill-chosen word, a false inflection . . . She wished Colin and his friend would return. Willingly as she had stepped into the breach this evening, she was anxious to shed the responsibility at the earliest moment and return to her mother, who might be having a fit of the sulks at being left.

A business function, Colin had said vaguely on the phone. When Sally had arrived, neither he nor his friend Eva had been dressed for a social event of any formality, but then, nowadays that was usual. The more glittering the occasion, the shabbier the attire, it seemed. Sally had asked no questions. Back by ten, they had promised. If they were delayed, they would call her. She hoped they would keep their word.

At three minutes past ten, as Sally was dozing, she heard the sound of the front-door key.

Yawning and stretching, she went outside to greet them. Eva's appearance was much as it had been when she left: casual, self-possessed. Her companion looked entirely different, for the good reason that it was not Colin. After a swift double-take, Sally advanced with a politely questioning look. Eva, who was removing her coat, flashed her a smile.

'Not late, are we? We drove as fast as we dared. Colin not back yet?'

'No. Should he be?' A glance at the newcomer showed Sally a sandy-haired man of wiry build who seemed ill at ease. He was avoiding her gaze as if anxious to by-pass the tedious business of introduction. His clothes were even more informal than Colin's had been. Turning, Eva made a half-playful adjustment to the zip of his leather jacket.

'I'd have thought so, but he may have been held up. He had to leave early to see the sergeant at the police station.'

'Oh, I see. About Louise?'

'I gather so. Apparently Colin had something to tell him. So I told him to take the car and got Jock to bring me home. My brother, Jock . . . Sally Wentworth. Sally's a friend of Mrs Fletcher's. She very kindly stood in for us this evening.'

Sally offered a hand. As if noticing her for the first time, Eva's brother with manifest reluctance took it limply in his own. The skin felt tepid, sweaty. 'Pleased to know you,' he muttered through clenched teeth.

The feeling, Sally decided, wasn't mutual. 'The fire's still alive . . . just,' she informed his sister. 'The children have been angels. Have a good time?'

'Marvellous, thanks. Jock won't agree.' Eva gave her brother a comic scowl. 'He doesn't like that sort of thing. But he makes a useful navigator. We're so grateful to you, Sally. You'll be wanting to get home to your mother.' Fishing a pound note from her purse, she proffered it. 'Something towards the petrol.'

Sally waved it aside. 'Don't be silly. What are friends for? I'll say good night, then. Tell Colin I was sorry not to see him again.'

'I will. Is this your coat? Let me just . . . Fits nicely, doesn't it, across the shoulders? Suits you. Okay—got everything? Jock, open the door for Sally. Mind how you drive back. 'Night.'

Her mother was awake but not fretful. 'I've done the *Guardian* crossword,' she proclaimed, flourishing the newspaper. 'Well, all but two. I believe the clues are wrong. Did your friends get back all right?'

'Prompt to time. At least . . .'

Old Mrs Wentworth was not one to be fobbed off. She peered up from her orthopaedic cushion. 'At least what?'

'Nothing. Only that Colin didn't come back, himself. Eva's brother brought her home instead.'

Her mother's lips pursed. 'Her *brother?*'

'I think I could see a family resemblance.' Folding the *Guardian*, Sally inspected her mother's water jug. 'Anyway it's no business of mine.'

'It ought to be someone's business. Two children there in the house with them.'

'I've no reason to . . .' Sally paused, thinking about it. 'I must admit, I took what she said at face value. Though it is odd, now that I look back. Before they went, Colin said nothing about seeing the police. The impression I got was that they were simply going to this party, or whatever, and would both be coming straight back.'

'Police?' her mother echoed keenly.

'Eva said he'd gone off by himself to speak to one of the officers investigating Louise's disappearance. It must have been arranged beforehand, unless . . .'

'Unless what?' Mrs Wentworth had dealt for too long with her daughter's introspective pauses to concern herself with subtlety.

'I did have a call from someone called Ferrari. He seemed to want to talk to Colin. Perhaps he managed to contact him at the party, and told him something. Oh well.' Sally took the jug into the bathroom next door for a refill. When she came back, her mother was gazing dreamily at a porcelain plaque, a family heirloom, attached to the facing wall.

'I'd give the station a ring,' she said suddenly, 'if I were in your shoes.'

'What?' Sally looked up, startled, from stretching cling-film over the rim of the jug.

'Talk to that officer. Ask him if this Colin has been in to see him.'

'Why on earth should I do that? It's no concern of mine.'

'Then why tell me about it?'

'It's just an item of interest. Not important. I only mentioned it because . . .' Once more Sally reached a crevasse in her thinking. 'I don't know,' she said finally, 'and I really don't care. They'll have to sort out their own problems. *I've* no say in the matter.'

Old Mrs Wentworth lay looking at her as she moved around the bed, collecting oddments that mysteriously had accumulated in the course of the evening. 'You always were one,' she said presently, in apparent idleness, 'for shelving things. How many holidaymakers have you left stranded, I wonder, for want of a phone call at the right time?'

Sally curbed her irritation. 'I've only ever had one genuine complaint. And that turned out to be the fault of the hotelier.'

'This could be the fault of someone else.'

'What could?'

'Whatever it is you're in a stew about,' her mother retorted. 'You ring that station number. Where's the harm?'

'Mother, you're impossible. Have you taken your tablets? I thought not. I'll get them.'

Discovering the phial in the kitchen, Sally picked it up and stood looking at it, seeing not its contents but other, unidentifiable things on the borders of her own consciousness. She started to return to the bedroom. Instead of arriving there, she found herself stationary in the hall alongside the telephone, her fingers on the receiver administering small restless taps. With a hiss of impatience she came away, halted, went back, seized the local directory. Flipping pages, she found the number and dialled.

A deep voice answered. With her lips buried in the mouthpiece, as she had seen it done in TV police series, she asked softly for Sergeant Dawson.

'Beg pardon, madam?'

'Sergeant Dawson,' she repeated clearly, capitulating. She pictured her mother, hugging herself gleefully under the sheet. 'Is it possible to have a word with him?'

' 'Fraid he's not on duty. Anyone else help you?'

'What time did he go off?'

'Noon yesterday,' the voice said patiently. 'Something I can do?'

'Has Mr Fletcher called in? If so, can you tell me if he's still there?'

'*Fletcher?* Don't believe we've had anyone of that name. Wait a bit. Are we talking about the gentleman in the missing mother case . . . her ex-husband?'

'That's right,' said Sally, a little breathless. 'I understand he was due to see one of the investigating officers some time this evening.'

'By appointment?'

'I'm not sure.'

'Hold on a second. I'll put you through to D.I. Cummings. He's in charge of the case.'

As the climax to sundry squawks and buzzings, a fresh male voice at baritone pitch rapped its name down the wire. Seized by the urge to hang up, Sally overcame it heroically.

'I'm sorry, Inspector, if I'm wasting your time. I'm inquiring on behalf of a friend.'

'Yes?' The syllable was uttered neutrally. As concisely as possible she explained the circumstances, half-affronted, half-intimidated by the dead silence at the other end, a silence that endured until the instant that she finished speaking, at which point Detective-Inspector Cummings, without fuss, took over.

'So you're wondering why he should have said he was looking in to see us, if he wasn't?'

'I'm wondering why I was *told* he was doing so. Am I being rather silly?'

'Probably,' he agreed disarmingly. 'Let's hope so, eh? I'm just having another glance at the file, Miss Wentworth . . .' A faint whistling became audible; it sounded like the Toreador's Song from *Carmen*. 'You say you're a friend of Colin Fletcher's,' he resumed eventually. 'Have you known him long?'

'Actually I hardly know him at all. It's Louise Fletcher I've been friendly with.'

'Were you surprised by her disappearance?'

She hesitated. 'Yes and no. She hadn't been quite herself the week previously, but as I told your sergeant, she wasn't the type to—'

'Hold it a moment, Miss Wentworth, will you? I've a call on the other line.'

Fidgeting, she waited while a subdued murmuring reached her ear from the inspector's invisible office. She was beginning to regret, if not resent, her mother's advice to make the call. She could almost hear the comments being bandied about the police station. 'Some middle-aged spinster lady . . . all fired up over her boyfriend . . . thinks he's fallen prey to the Mafia . . . Chief's fobbing her off now . . .' She should never have dreamt of interfering. Outsiders had enough on their plates, and besides . . . On the point of cutting the connection, Sally heard the 'ting' of a bell, followed by the renewed voice of Inspector Cummings, sharpened—was it her fancy?—by a note of urgency. 'Still there, Miss Wentworth?'

'I'm here. Look, I know you're a busy man, Inspector, and I'm sure you've better things to do than—'

'Good. I was afraid you might have run off. Tell me. Does the name Ferrari mean anything to you?'

CHAPTER 14

The blackness was Stygian. It was like being immersed in a giant pot of ink with the cap screwed tight. He could hear Louise's breathing. There was a faintly rasping quality to it, as though she were asthmatic. As far as he knew, she had never suffered in that way. Groping, he rearranged his overcoat around her, trying to ensure that she was warm.

He had no means of gauging her condition. Once the door had clumped shut, leaving them in darkness, there was little he could do. Unusually, he was out of matches. He had meant to buy a fresh box that day, but other events had driven it out of his mind. The previous evening he had searched the kitchen drawer where normally they were kept, but none had been left: Eva must have neglected to restock. His sole resource was to talk softly at intervals to Louise, ask how she felt, if she was in pain; this, vainly, was what he had been doing for at least an hour.

He tried once more. 'Louise? Can you hear? It's me, Colin. Are you able to—'

'I *hear* you.' To his vast relief, a trace of irritability was detectable in the weak reply. 'Do you have to keep on?'

'I was afraid you weren't . . . feeling so good.'

'Just dozed off, that's all.' There was a silence. 'Had a rotten dream.'

During another extended hiatus she seemed to have been gathering her thoughts. 'I dreamt I'd killed a man. He was lying there, bleeding . . . What are you doing here? Where are the children?'

'They're fine. Sally's with them.'

'Sal?' She gave this lengthy consideration. The gap in her teeth was causing her sibilants to be accompanied by a faint whistling. 'What does she know about kids?'

'She's just keeping an eye on them. She can cope until we get back.'

Fletcher awaited the next question. It arrived predictably. 'Where the hell are we?'

'I can't get the door open,' he explained, matter-of-fact. 'It's jammed.'

'Thump on it, then. Make someone hear.'

'I've tried. No one seems to be around.'

'Where is it, exactly? It's so damn dark in here . . .'

'Lie still. You'll bring on a headache.'

'It's here already.' He heard the gasp that was wrung out of her as she sat up. 'God, my brain . . . It's coming apart. I don't understand any of this. I was . . .'

A further pause: an eloquent one in the darkness. 'Are we still in that attic? If this has something to do with you, Colin, you bastard, I'll never . . . What have you done with the kids? I'll get them back, you hear? If you think I'm sitting down tamely under this, you must be—'

'Will you shut up?' In the silence that rather unexpectedly ensued, he added, 'It wasn't me. Someone I thought I knew took advantage. We've got to get out of here.'

'Where's *here?* I can't see a hand in front of my eyes.'

'We're in a kind of basement room at the farmhouse. If you remember—'

'Of course I remember.' She still sounded tetchy rather than scared. 'They've been keeping me since . . . What day is it?'

'Never mind. The essential thing is to find a way out. There has to be one. You weren't in here before, by any chance?'

'Search me. Can't we force the door?'

'It was built for a fortress. I'm wondering if there's a window of any sort.'

'A basement, you said.'

'Could be only partial. If there's a fanlight, obviously it'll be near the ceiling. I'll have to prod around with something. Stay put. There are some tools the other side.'

Rising stiffly, he flexed his limbs, took a few tentative paces into the encompassing ink. At the fifth step he fell over a potato sack. His left hand struck the side of the wheelbarrow. Louise said sharply, 'What are you up to?'

'Not up—down.' Scrambling to his feet, Fletcher toppled backwards over another sack. This time he subsided with a grunt on to a bag of peat. At the third attempt, feeling his way, he contrived to reach the further wall: his arrival became apparent when his shoulder biffed something and set it jangling. Reaching up, he gouged his thumb on the point of a projection and swore under his breath.

When he lifted the tool down, he was able to identify it as a scythe. Planting it carefully at the base of the wall, he fumbled to the right, encountered something that swung away and then back, smiting his wrist painfully before he could seize it, bring it down to floor level, trace its outline. A pitchfork. Lifting it vertically, he felt the prongs touch the plaster. He began taking short steps to his right, tapping wall and ceiling.

'Now what?' Louise demanded.

'Don't budge, or I'll tread on you. If there's an opening anywhere, this should find it.'

'The door would be simpler,' she said crossly. 'There must be a way of slipping the catch.'

'Try to find it,' he growled, intent on his task.

To his annoyance, he realized a moment later that she was taking him at his word. A scrabbling sound was followed by a blow to his ribs as she cannoned into him, sending him off balance. The pitchfork swayed dangerously. Bringing it under control, he said with restraint, 'I told you not to move. Why don't you do as I say?'

'If I'd avoided doing what other people said,' she countered, breaking clear of him, 'I wouldn't be in this fix. From here on I'm listening to myself and no one else, thank you very kindly. Carry on looking for your window. I'd sooner go out the way I came in.'

'Can't say I'm that choosy. As long as we get out, any way will do.'

'You don't sound too optimistic.'

A new note was perceptible in her voice. It struck him that, until now, in her estimation he had remained the villain of the piece, the root cause of all that had occurred. His unpremeditated remark had ignited, possibly, fresh fires in her mind. He thought more carefully about his next words.

'All we need is a spot of coordination. If we each try to do things in our own way . . .'

'Old habits die hard.' He couldn't make out whether she was being tart or humorous; or both. 'Got anything to suggest?'

'Just let me finish. If I find nothing, it's your turn. Agreed?'

She said nothing, but evidently remained still while he continued to poke with the pitchfork, without result. Having completed the circuit of the room, he lowered the scythe to the floor behind the potato sacks and stood for a moment removing the dirt specks that had fallen into his eyes. Out of the darkness, Louise said, 'Nothing?'

'Seemingly not,' he admitted. 'Off you go.'

Seconds later, he heard her scraping at the door. Although logic told him it was futile, he found himself hoping that she might yet achieve something feminine and miraculous, obtaining release with a flick of cool fingers and a calm 'Shall we be leaving?' in the finest tradition of fictional escapology. It didn't happen. What she did say, several times, was something brief and uncomplimentary about doors with no interior handles and a surfeit of mass. Presently came a series of soft thuds. He said placatingly, 'No point in that. You'll hurt yourself.'

'That'll be a change.'

Groping for the pitchfork, Fletcher took it across and joined her at the door, feeling momentarily the pressure of her shoulder before she edged away. 'Close-fitting,' he confirmed, having explored the woodwork with his fingertips, 'but we might get the prongs of this thing into a crack somewhere. Stand clear.'

'Aim for the catch.' She spoke from a point away to his left.

'I'm not sure just where it is. Have to chance my arm.'

At first he proceeded tentatively, insinuating the tips of the prongs into what he deemed to be the join of door and frame, then exerting lateral pressure. Each time, the steel slid free abortively. At last, taking blind aim, he thumped the implement against the planks, repeated the action until it felt as though he had achieved some penetration, then swung with all his strength on the haft. A loud crack rang through the storeroom. Louise said excitedly, 'Done it?'

'Yes,' he replied bitterly. 'Snapped the bloody pitchfork. Hang about while I feel for something else.'

'I'm not going anywhere.'

If he had to be immured with someone else in a hole in the ground, Fletcher reflected while hunting for a substitute weapon, he could easily have fared worse for a partner. Many a female would by now have been reduced to a hysterical heap, impervious to reason. For that matter, so would a number of males of his acquaintance. Considering what she had lived through already, Louise—as near as he could judge from the sound of her—was facing up admirably to what was fast becoming a situation fraught with imponderables. He wondered about her mental state. Was she aware, even now, that she had in fact killed a man? He suspected that she still thought of it, if at all, as a nightmare. To keep her mind occupied, he launched a running commentary as he searched.

'Every damn object you can think of, except what we really need—a stick of dynamite. There's something parked in the corner that feels like a motor-mower, would you believe? Wide-headed broom . . . shovel . . . long-handled scythe . . .'

'Why not the scythe?'

'Wrong shape. No purchase. The shovel might be better, only it's got raised edges that would stop it going into the frame. For God's sake! There has to be something.'

'If you could start the mower, couldn't we attach a rope, fasten the other end to the door . . .'

'We don't have a rope,' he explained gently. 'Nor any means of fixing it. Furthermore the motor wouldn't be strong enough. Apart from all that, I can't see a bloody thing I'm doing inside this cocoon . . . if I tried to start it, I'd probably sever a hand. The wheelbarrow, now. That might make more sense.'

'How?'

'Trouble is, it's a lightweight. What we need—'

'Can't we fill it?'

'Huh?'

'Load the barrow with something heavy. Then use it as a ram.'

'We could try,' he said, after a pause. The idea, he knew, was a non-starter, but it would keep them busy. 'The potato sacks are probably best. They'll tend to stay in place. Where are you, at the moment?'

'Left side of the door.'

'Move well back. I'll get the barrow lined up, then fill it with junk.'

Half-rotten though the potatoes undoubtedly were, each sack weighed something like fifty pounds. Piling the wheelbarrow with as many as was practicable, Fletcher raised the grips experimentally, felt the load sway, put it down, did some redistributing. Then he felt his way over to the door and back again. Holding the direction in his mind, he lifted the wheelbarrow, tensed himself. 'Keep still,' he said. 'I'm trying now.'

In the blackness, it was impossible to estimate the moment of impact. He simply ran the makeshift juggernaut full tilt and braced himself for the shock.

When it came, the pain forked through the sinew of wrists and shoulders like an electrical charge, exploding the grips out of his fingers. The barrow fell sideways, evacuating its contents. From her corner, Louise ventured a comment.

'Judging by the groans, that wasn't a success.'

'We'll never do it that way.' Fletcher nursed his abrasions.

'One more try.'

Cursing to himself, he retrieved the sacks, reloaded the barrow, took sightless aim once more. This time he released the grips prematurely. Delivering what sounded like a glancing blow, the unguided missile again collapsed to the floor. Fletcher gave up. 'You might as well chuck peanuts at a battle tank. We'll have to think of something else.'

'Why don't we just sit and wait for them to come back?'

'We don't know how long that might be.' How convincing did he sound? Smoothly he added, 'Those cuts and bruises of yours need attention.'

'I shan't peg out for the sake of a few hours. They've never yet left me alone for more than half a day. When they do show up . . .'

'Yes?'

'Well, there are two of us. We should be able to work something out.'

Fletcher thought long and hard about his answer. Finally he said, 'Maybe you're right. We'll wait on events. Sure to check up on us, aren't they, in the morning?'

The sound that aroused him was not one that he could readily identify. His impression was that, although half-dozing, he had been obscurely conscious of it for some considerable time. Its nature was perplexing, and yet disturbingly familiar. Having listened for a few moments, he sat up on the peat bags and spoke in an undertone, but distinctly.

'Awake, Louise?'

'This is hardly the place for a restful night. What's that noise?'

'You can hear it too. How long has it been going on?'

'Quite some while. What can it be, do you think?'

'Sounds a bit like murky weather outside,' he ventured, after a pause. 'That's encouraging.'

'In what way?'

'If we can hear that, it means there has to be some kind of outlet that I've missed. Perhaps part of the ceiling . . .'

'Doesn't sound like weather to me,' said Louise.

They sat listening.

'An air vent,' exclaimed Fletcher. 'That must be it. A storeroom would have one, of course.'

'So why didn't you find it?'

'Shielded, probably. I'll have another poke around.'

He started to get up. Out of the blackness to his right came a gasp. He said apprehensively, 'What is it?'

'I seem to have stuck my foot in a puddle.'

'I thought it was totally dry in here. Water in your shoe?'

'A basinful.'

'Take it off. Your stocking, too. You musn't get chilled. I'll just be—'

Fletcher's words died in his throat. In taking a step off the peat bags down to floor level, he had created a splash. Moisture now assailed his foot and ankle. Withdrawing hastily to higher ground, he dropped to a crouch and explored with a hand. Water to a depth of inches engulfed his fingers. It was ice-cold.

For a matter of seconds he kept silent. He could hear the slightly emphasized breathing of Louise as she peeled off her stocking. The background noise that had aroused them was insistent. Thoughts careered through his brain, jostling for priority.

He rediscovered his voice. 'I think we may have a small problem on our hands.'

'Problem?' Louise sounded preoccupied.

'It's not just a puddle,' he said carefully. 'The entire floor seems to be under water.'

There was a silence to match the darkness. When Louise spoke again, her voice was rigidly under control. 'Does that mean it *is* rain we can hear? And it's getting in somewhere?'

'Could be.'

'What other explanation is there?'

They listened again to the sound. It was like the tinkling of a rill over rocks. 'I believe,' said Fletcher, 'it might be coming from the steps outside.'

'Are they exposed to the rain?'

'I wouldn't have thought so.'

'You're right,' she said, after another interval of ear-straining. 'It's definitely from outside the door. The water must be seeping underneath. How uncomfortable.'

'Keep on the sacks,' Fletcher warned her. 'I'll hand across a couple more. This is one instance, I feel, where it's better to find yourself in the fertilizer.'

A smothered giggle reached him. He couldn't recall the last time he had struck a laugh out of Louise. Beyond that, she had never been in the habit of informing him that he was right about anything. Abruptly, despite everything, he felt oddly buoyant.

'It's not rainwater, is it?' Accepting the extra bags from him, she put the question sedately.

'I can't imagine what else—'

'Can't you? Look, there's no need to be strong and manly about it. If rain got in here, the place would be permanently damp. This is the first soaking it's had, that's obvious. And the fact that we're here can hardly be coincidence, right?'

'Unlikely,' he conceded reluctantly.

'So, what's causing it? A tap left running?'

'Maybe. I dare say they took off in a rush.'

Notwithstanding the darkness, he could almost see the crinkling of Louise's nose and forehead. 'Took off?' she repeated presently. 'You think they've done a bunk?'

'In a manner of speaking. Eva's pretty smart. If she thought they could—'

'Eva?' Before he could reply, Louise went swiftly on. 'Somebody took advantage . . . isn't that what you said? Is it this Eva you were talking about?'

'I was taken for a ride,' he said shortly. 'Got those sacks under you?'

'Never mind about me, I'm fine. It's Eva I want to hear about. Who is she? How did she get her claws into you? What made you think she—'

'All right, Louise, give it a rest. We're not married any more, in case you've forgotten.'

'Colin W. Fletcher, you need your head examined. You must be the easiest meat in the Midlands.'

'You've not been doing so well yourself, just lately.'

'How about calling it quits for the moment?' she suggested, after a humming pause. 'There's a more immediate problem to be tackled. If what you say is right, somehow we've got to find a way out of here. We can't drift around on peat bags for days on end.'

Fletcher said nothing. As if tuned to his cerebral waveband, she added, 'Or am I skirting the issue?'

'It's hard to say. They didn't take me into their—'

'A short while ago you were sure they'd be turning up again in the morning. Have you changed your mind?'

'One can't be certain of anything. I simply don't know.'

'One thing,' Louise said presently, 'I do know.'

'What's that?'

'The water level's rising.'

Fletcher extended a probing foot. The splash came earlier than he had hoped. He said casually, 'I'll go along with that analysis. Are you still high and dry?'

'Relatively. You know, it can't be an ordinary household tap. It's too fast.'

'Maybe they've diverted a stream.'

'Fixed up a hose, more likely. There's a hydrant outside, in the yard. I saw it.'

'You might be right.' Yielding to the inevitable, Fletcher threw aside any attempt to keep her out of the picture. 'There's certainly more coming down than you'd expect from a kitchen sink. I think it may not be a bad idea to start stacking more of this garbage in the corner. Then we can both get well clear of the water. How about it?'

'Whatever you say, boss.'

'If you want to help, you can pass me those top sacks you're standing on. After that, give me your wrist and I'll hoist you across. Watch yourself—don't fall. If either of us gets drenched, we're in double trouble. Let me know when the first sack's on its way.'

'Here it comes.'

'Okay, got it. Now the other. Good. Let's have your hand.'

Amid the blackness, their fingers met. Closing his firmly about her forearm, Fletcher said, 'A yard or so, I reckon. Jump when I tell you. Ready? Now!'

Her body struck his, pitching him sideways. Recovering, he clutched her until they were both steady. To his surprise, she felt not taut but limp: he could feel the irregular pounding of her heart. 'You know,' he said, 'there's nothing to be alarmed about. Once the water finds its level, it'll stop rising.'

'Naturally,' she said, and broke away. He heard her clawing at a potato sack alongside the wall.

Rejoining her cautiously, he lent his strength to the operation and together they heaved it to the right, hearing it splash down in the corner. More sacks followed it, until they were marooned on a small mound with barely room for both of them. Working blind, Fletcher had done his best to construct the sanctuary in pyramidical fashion, with steps: how far he had succeeded, it was difficult to assess. He touched Louise's arm.

'Hop across.'

'Have we used all we can?'

'Any higher and we'll hit the ceiling. Tread with care.'

He waited tensely, guessing at her movements. At the conclusion of a series of scratching noises mingled with soft thuds, she said breathlessly, 'I'm *in situ* . . . I think. Now give me *your* hand. Unless you're too chauvinistic to accept help from a female.'

'I'm on my way.'

Supported by the angle of the walls, the hand-made hillock was as firm as could be expected. Installing himself at Louise's side, Fletcher sat silently for a while, listening to the continued faint splashing from the steps outside. The potatoes were too far gone to be knobbly. Under their weight, it felt as if they were disintegrating, contracting into pulp. Hooking his glasses more securely on to his ears, he found a new position for his right hip, just in contact with her left one.

She didn't edge off. Doubtless there was no room for her to move. He blinked several times, in the absurd hope that his pupils might yet adjust and focus on something. A sigh came from Louise. It sounded involuntary, a product of partial release of tension. It sounded feminine. Shifting his foot an inch, he touched her ankle.

'I did remember to tell you?' he said. 'The children are fine.'

CHAPTER 15

Thumbing the bellpush a third time, Police Constable Ivor Jenkins squinted at his colleague. 'Heavy sleepers,' he remarked.

'Either that, or . . .' Taking a few paces backwards out of the porch, the other constable looked up at the front of the house. 'Still no light,' he reported. 'We could sling gravel at one of the top windows.'

'Wait while I check back.' Returning to the car, Jenkins called up the station. 'We've rung at the house,' he said, 'but we can't raise an answer. No sign of a light. What do we do?'

'Any sound of movement inside?' asked Inspector Cummings.

'No, sir.'

'Any sign of a car?'

'Nothing in the driveway. Garage door is locked.'

'You've knocked as well as rung?'

'Loud enough to—'

'Wake the dead? All right, Constable. You have my authority to break in. Do it quietly. I'd prefer it if the neighbours weren't alerted.'

'Using our lower teeth and our fingernails,' Jenkins announced on his return to the porch, 'we're to smash down the door.' He eyed the lock. 'Alternatively . . . Got a plastic credit card on you?'

'There's nobody in the house,' Cummings informed the bulky, dark-haired figure seated hunch-shouldered in the ante-room to his office. 'The children have gone. Likewise a few of their belongings, by the look of it. Any idea of her home address, this Eva Maynard?'

Ferrari shook his head. 'Not offhand, but she'd be in the book. I can tell you where her brother lives.'

The inspector glanced up from the directory he had seized and opened. 'He's the one with a daughter of eleven?' Ferrari nodded. 'House or flat? Town house. Biggish? Four bedrooms. Hm. Give us the map reference, will you. Then I want you to—'

'Inspector. Are you planning to raid both addresses?'

'I'm intending to pay them exploratory visits. Why?'

'I'd like to come along. I guess I'm entitled.

'I've got to admit,' Cummings said slowly, 'if you hadn't taken the trouble to call us tonight . . . Why did you, incidentally?'

'I told you. I wanted to find out whether Fletcher had gone to you with the information I gave him.'

'What made you think he might not have?'

Ferrari shrugged. The inspector studied him for a moment. 'Okay,' he said. 'Button your jacket. The spare muscle might come in handy.'

In the car, he said to the investigator, 'You're convinced Mrs Fletcher has been abducted?'

'Starts to look like it, doesn't it? Now it's her kids gone, as well.'

Cummings whistled a theme from *Tosca*, broke off in mid-phrase. 'What's your reading of the situation?'

'I just have this feeling,' Ferrari said weightily, 'I may have been taken for a ride.'

'By the husband?'

'Who else? He's the one been acting the injured innocent party, and giving a sound performance. But it could have been some kind of double bluff. I'm not sure.'

The brows of the inspector merged into a furrowed line. 'I understood he hired you to get evidence?'

'Right, he did. But what if he'd other ideas all along? Could be, he teamed up with this Maynard woman and they hatched this plot whereby she and her brother snatched the kids while he seemed to be doing his best, via yours truly, to protect 'em. Then later, when the heat came off . . .'

'He should know,' Cummings said grimly, 'that in cases like this, the heat's never off.'

'Sure, but people don't think of that, do they? Not when they're obsessed parents. They've just the one thought in their minds. As long as they do what they have to, then sod the consequences. But if it comes to that,' Ferrari added, blocking the inspector's interjection, 'his planning could have been meticulous, for all we know. They might have it all sewn up. Fake passports, plane tickets to Rio . . . the works. They could all be out of the country right now, the lot of them.'

'Not too likely, Mr Ferrari.'

'Where disputed families are involved, it's the unlikely things that tend to happen. You know that.'

'If I didn't,' agreed Cummings, 'we wouldn't be sitting here, bouncing around at twelve-thirty a.m. en route to a pair of dwelling places we've never heard of.'

'Which address are you taking first?'

The inspector smiled thinly. 'We do still adopt basic techniques in the Force, I'll have you know. That carload behind—' He jerked a thumb. 'They'll turn off shortly for Mrs Maynard's flat. They'll take up position, but they'll do nothing until I give the signal. Happy?'

Ferrari grunted. 'I think we've forgotten something.'

'What?' Cummings stiffened.

'Fletcher's been living somewhere since his divorce. I've always contacted him at his office, but unless he was shacked up with his Eva from the start he'll have had some address of his own, won't he? If I'm right about him, that's where they could be now, him and Eva and the kids.'

Cummings buried his face. 'I'm getting a bit fazed by

the various possibilities. How about Mrs Fletcher? What's become of her?'

'There's this farmhouse of the brother's. That's another possibility. She could be—'

'I've not forgotten. But I want to eliminate those other places first. If we get results, we may not have to bother with farmhouses thirty miles from here.' As a fork junction showed itself ahead, he glanced over a shoulder. 'There they go. Another ten minutes and we might learn something.'

The street in Abingmore containing Jock Deedes's town house was choked on both sides with parked vehicles. At the inspector's bidding, the driver pulled up fifty yards short and the car's five other occupants clambered out, the sergeant and a constable heading for a side-street which led to the rear of the block, while Cummings and another constable, with Ferrari in tow, made quietly for the street entrance. When the three of them were assembled on the unlit doorstep, the inspector spoke softly into his personal radio and received an acknowledgement from the sergeant. Then he stood looking along the street.

Presently the police car's sidelamps winked twice. He gave a snort of satisfaction. 'Green light from the Maynard's place.' Lifting the door knocker, he rapped three times.

After a brief delay a light went on in the hall. Cummings raised a warning hand to the constable, poised to throw his weight at the door. Almost immediately it was opened from behind. A sandy-haired man in a bathrobe stood blinking at them. 'Something wrong?'

'Mr Deedes? Jock Deedes?'

'That's me. What are you lot doing here, this time of night? I never phoned for the law.'

Cummings said pleasantly, 'Mind if we step inside?'

'Without knowing your business—'

'Missing persons inquiry,' the inspector explained, shouldering past him. "Where's the telephone?'

'Down there, back of the hall. Who's missing?'

'I'd have thought you'd have known that. From your sister.'

'Eva? What does she have to do with it?'

The four of them were now crammed into the hall, which was long but narrow. Hot air gusted from vents. 'Cosy in here,' remarked Cummings. 'Always have your heating full on, do you, in the early hours? Seems a mite extravagant.'

'We enjoy our comfort, my daughter and me. If it's any concern of yours. What's this all about?'

At a signal from his superior, the constable strode through to the back of the house, flinging open doors. Receiving a nod, Ferrari trotted upstairs. Deedes, stationary in the hall, eyed the activity in a pensive manner.

'I hope you've some authority, Superintendent, for what you're doing. Else I'll have you.'

'Thanks for the promotion. Authority? I've all I need. Know anything about a Mrs Louise Fletcher?'

'Never heard of her. If she's the one that's missing, she's not here. It's just me and my daughter. I don't welcome house guests—especially female ones. Ask anyone.'

'The person we'd like to ask is your sister. Been in touch with her recently?'

'You keep on about Eva. Depends what you call recent. We communicate from time to time. What's he doing upstairs? My Hilary's going to be scared out of her wits.'

'Kids go crazy over him. Know somebody called Miss Sally Wentworth?'

'Sorry.'

'That's odd. According to her, you and she were introduced just a few hours ago.'

'Then whoever she is, she's a liar. I've been here all

evening. Ask Hilary.'

'You've not been with your sister?'

'Here we go again. No, as it so happens, I've not seen a lot of Eva just lately. Look, is she okay? I'm not wild about the way her name keeps cropping up. Nothing's happened to her, has it?'

'Shall we make a deal?' Cummings suggested. 'You tell me if anything's happened to Mrs Fletcher: I'll tell you ditto regarding your sister. Can't say fairer.'

The left side of Deedes's face developed a twitch. 'Sounds one-sided to me. You can deliver, I can't. How am I supposed to know about this Fletcher dame?'

'When, exactly, did you last have physical contact with your sister?'

'I don't recall.'

'Short memories you motor-dealers have. Miss Wentworth saw you together, you and Eva, just this evening.'

'Did she now?'

'At the home of Mrs Fletcher. Where her two children were upstairs, asleep.'

Deedes looked back at him in silence. The inspector added helpfully, 'They're not there now. The children, I mean. Can you explain that?'

'Maybe they went for a midnight hike. Look, if you're so interested in my sister, why don't you talk to her? She's got a flat the other side of town. I can give you the address.'

'Not necessary, thanks. We shall probably—'

The telephone rang from the rear of the hall. 'Probably for me,' Cummings said politely, outstripping Deedes across the carpet and arriving first. Lifting the receiver, he listened.

'Right,' he said. 'No, stick around for a bit. I'll let you know.' He hung up. 'Speak of the devil,' he remarked. 'That was a message, would you credit it, from your sister's residence. She's not there. So we wouldn't have reached her that way, would we?'

'No law against being out for the night. I think she's got a bloke.'

'Mentioned him, has she?'

'She may have done, in passing.'

'Of course, you wouldn't know the first thing about him. Who he is, or anything corny like that?'

'Eva keeps her private life to herself. I'm not interested.'

'No, you wouldn't be. Cars. They're your interest—right, Mr Deedes? I hear you run a Datsun. Got it bedded down for the night?'

'It's in dock for repairs.'

'Oh, tough luck. Still, you won't object if we take a look inside your garage here? Routine check.'

'Not without a warrant you don't.'

'Why not? Got something to hide?'

'Just my privacy.'

'We've already intruded on that. Surely your garage is less sensitive?'

'I've had a bellyful of this. I'm calling my lawyer.'

'Go right ahead.' Cummings stood aside.

As Deedes started to dial, the inspector kept his gaze on the handset while he spoke into his radio. 'Get round here, will you, Sergeant? Small job for you.' Taking out a notepad, he jotted something quickly down before stepping back to remove the receiver from the motor-dealer's grasp.

'Here!' expostulated Deedes. 'What the—'

'Save it,' Cummings advised. 'If that really was your solicitor you were about to call, I'll apologize later.' Consulting his pad, he took up the receiver again. 'With your permission.' He dialled the operator, waited patiently for a response. 'Detective-Inspector Leslie Cummings speaking,' he announced on an official note.

'Bancester CID. I have a number here for which I'd like a name and address. Can you tell me how I go about obtaining it?'

On Ferrari's return from the upper floors, the inspector and Deedes were seated in silence, facing one another, in the dealer's study, observed from the open doorway by the constable who had arrived from the rear. Cummings glanced up inquiringly. Ferrari said, 'The girl's up there in bed, by herself. No trace of anyone else.'

Deedes stirred. 'If you've been putting the frighteners on my daughter . . .'

'Shut up,' the inspector said placidly. 'Get anything out of her?'

'She says her dad's been here all evening. But she's hazy on detail.'

'You wouldn't be that sharp if a man burst into your bedroom and—'

'I'm sure Mr Ferrari tapped and walked in, like the gentleman he is. Make a search?'

'Every room and cupboard.'

'Go over the place again. Bates here will give you a hand.'

Ferrari vanished with the constable. The look that Deedes turned upon the inspector was loaded to the point of explosion. 'You enjoy this, don't you? Midnight harassment. Right down your street.'

'Sooner be tucked up in bed, myself,' Cummings said mildly. 'Night shifts are a vastly overrated . . . Ah, Sergeant. Get inside all right? Find anything?'

'Yes, sir. A very nice Sierra, metallic-brown, this year's model.' The sergeant, a man of modest stature but impressive girth, stood in the doorway with a dirt streak down one side of his face. Cummings glanced admonishingly at Deedes.

'You told me your car was in dock.'

'The Datsun is. That's a spare I've been using.'

'Wouldn't have occurred to you to mention that, of course. You've not used it tonight?'

'Hasn't been driven for twenty-four hours.'

'Sir, the rad's still warm.'

Cummings bent another look, fuller still of reproach, on the dealer, who said nothing. The sergeant added, 'Also, there's fresh mud splashed on the wings and bodywork. Wetter than spaghetti.' He produced a handkerchief to wipe his face. 'Stinks a bit, too.'

The inspector looked intrigued. 'Been driving across fields lately, Mr Deedes?'

'There's filth all over the roads, this time of year. Can I help it if I pick up the stuff as I go along?'

'No, I'm sure you can't. If you could, you'd have . . . Excuse me. Sounds like my call.'

Rising swiftly, Cummings went out to the hall. They heard him murmuring, then a more distinct 'Thank you, I'm greatly obliged. Sorry to have been a nuisance.' The receiver went down with a clash. 'Sergeant! Bring Mr Deedes along. Tell Bates to stay here with the girl, then you and her father join me in the car. Bring Ferrari.'

The car was already turned in the street when the three of them reached it. As they took off, Cummings said coolly from the front seat, 'If we're taking you for an unnecessary spin, Mr Deedes, you can sue us afterwards. Pending that, how about coming up with a direction or two? Save us a bit of time. No? Suit yourself. Headington Lane, Stroudbury,' he told the driver, peering out at signs. 'Get to the village, then we'll knock somebody up and ask.'

'I know Headington Lane,' said Ferrari. 'It's a turning off the main street, nearly opposite the Fox and Hounds.'

'Good. Does it stretch far?'

'Two or three miles.'

The inspector groaned. 'Let's hope to God there's a fat

nameplate for Silverbank Cottage.'

The car sped between hedgerows. Wedged between Ferrari and the sergeant, Deedes remained silent, gazing rigidly ahead. After a few miles they entered the fringes of the village, unlit and deserted. Ferrari leaned forward to point past the inspector's shoulder.

'There's the pub. Go just beyond it and take the turn to the left. Watch it, there's a nasty bend.'

Making the turn with aplomb, the driver reduced speed to a relative crawl while they stared out on both sides. 'A moon would have helped,' observed Cummings. 'Weave a bit, Doug. Aim your beams at the nameplates—if any. I suppose our friend back there still doesn't feel inclined to cooperate?'

'Get lost,' said the dealer.

'Not just to oblige you, we shan't. What's that over there? Little Oaks. This seems like the posh end. If Fletcher's been renting a place, he'd have picked somewhere cheap, I would guess.'

'Maybe we should ask,' suggested Ferrari.

'Keep going, Doug, for the moment. If we come to the end of the lane without spotting it, then we'll hammer on someone's door.'

At the foot of a gradient the lane went into a series of gentle curves, seemingly devoid of habitation. A dark mass of trees was discernible on each side. 'Forestry Commission land,' Ferrari muttered. 'Silverbank could be one of their tied cottages. If so . . . Is that a light along there?'

'Someone feeding a bonfire?' queried Cummings, after a moment's scrutiny. 'At two in the morning?'

'Hey!' Deedes had sat up. 'That's about where it is.'

'Step on it, Doug.'

As they approached, it became apparent that the blaze was at upper-floor level. Before the car had lurched to a halt, the inspector and Ferrari were out of the doors and sprinting for the gap in the blackthorn hedge, leaving the sergeant and driver to restrain a now distraught Deedes. With a yell, Ferrari called the inspector's attention to the cottage nameplate on a post as they charged through. Signifying assent, Cummings pointed to a minuscule upper window from which flames and smoke were gushing.

'Take it from the back,' he bawled, switching course. 'The ground rises. We might—'

'What's that?' Ferrari pulled up.

A movement to the right had caught his eye. From the gloom of a ragged shrubbery, a figure emerged into the glare. It was a small one, slow-moving and yet somehow purposeful. Dropping to one knee, Ferrari captured the fully-dressed little girl in a bear-hug. 'Are you Terri?'

She nodded, and turned to point. 'My brother's over there.'

Cummings, who had returned, leapt towards the shrubbery. Ferrari kept a tight grasp upon the girl. 'You're okay, the pair of you? Where's Mrs Maynard.'

'Eva's upstairs,' Terri told him, rubbing smoke out of her eyes. 'Me and my brother came out through the kitchen.'

The inspector reappeared, half-steering, half-hauling another slight figure clear of the bushes. 'We've got 'em both,' he said, relief sharp in his voice. 'How about the woman?'

'According to this one, she's still inside.'

With a bellowed order to his sergeant, who was already on his way, Cummings ran to the rear of the cottage and up the bank, bypassing the kitchen door from which smoke was starting to coil. The sergeant pursued him. Ferrari, clutching the girl, heard the smashing of glass; then for a while there was nothing but the roar and crackle from the roof. Presently he was joined by two other figures. Still grasped by the driver, Deedes was an unresisting hulk of hollow-eyed despair, open-mouthed but speechless. Receiving an interrogative glance from the policeman, Ferrari responded with a slight shrug.

'I've radioed for the appliance,' said the driver, maintaining his superfluous hold on the dealer.

'They'll need to be fast.' In an attempt to coax Terri away from the blaze and towards the car, Ferrari met resistance. She and her brother stood rooted, fixated by the spectacle. While he was considering what degree of persuasion was justified, an outline appeared at the top of the bank, slow-moving, carrying something. A second shape came into view, linked to the first by the burden. Together they staggered down the slope to garden level before setting down the load and wrapping it inside the greatcoat which the sergeant had peeled off. Extending an arm for Kevin, Ferrari held both children tightly.

'They've got her,' he told them. 'Now will you come back to the car?'

Black in the face and with watering eyes, the inspector detached himself from the heap on the ground and came over to where they stood. 'Help on its way?' he asked the driver, who nodded.

'Six to eight minutes, they said.'

'Doesn't matter,' Cummings said quietly. 'No particular rush.'

Deedes lurched forward as his knees gave way. Waving Ferrari off with the children, who now followed docilely, Cummings crouched to confront the dealer on level terms. 'Sorry, Mr Deedes,' he said clearly, 'but I'm afraid you've just lost your sister. Now will you tell us where you've been keeping Mrs Fletcher?'

CHAPTER 16

'How long has it been?'

'If I could see my watch-face, I'd come up with three-minute bulletins, if my glasses didn't need cleaning.'

'What became of the digital thing you had? The luminous one.'

'Flogged it. To help pay your damn maintenance.'

'I don't believe you.'

In the darkness he shrugged. 'Believe what you like. You always did.'

Expecting a comeback, he was answered by silence. When she spoke again, it was on the same key as before. 'How high is the water?'

He lowered a hand. 'Not much different,' he said bracingly, 'from last time. If at all. Maybe the flow has stopped.'

'Or else it's having to flood a wider area. So it's taking longer.'

'Optimist. Let's *assume* it's stopped. Then all we need do is cling to this rotten potato mountain until the Common Market grabs it for sale to the Third World. Then they'll find us.'

'Fried chips.' Her voice was husky. 'I could wolf a packet of them right now.'

'When we get out, I'll buy you a meal at Robbie's.'

'What with? According to you, I've had all your assets. God, I'm ravenous.'

'Cold?'

'Famished, freezing, frightened. No, cancel that last bit. Petrified.'

'Join the club.'

Presently she said, 'I was hoping it was just me.'

'Superman retired hurt after the divorce. How's the foot?'

'Dried off, but it's numb. I keep wiggling my toes.'

'Let's try some massage,' Fletcher suggested.

'We'll topple the sacks.'

'They're stable enough, I think. Give me your foot.'

Unwrapping it from his jacket, Louise slid it in his direction. At his touch she let out a small gasp, then remained tensely still while he rubbed the chilled flesh. 'Any improvement?' he asked.

'Not a lot, but it passes the odd minute. Who taught you this? The Maynard creature?'

'No,' he said, after a pause. 'I learned other lessons from her.'

'Similar to the ones I got from Rosenberg?'

'Like, not expecting too much from the opposite sex? Something on those lines. Boringly old-hat. It's a pity we have to keep mastering these ancient saws, over and over again. What's needed is a central computer bank of received wisdom, readily accessible to the . . . Is that any better?'

'If we ever get out of here, they may be able to save it.'

'We're going to get out.'

'Of course we are.'

'You don't believe me? I can't hear that splashing sound any more.'

'Me neither. But does it mean anything? Maybe the water level—'

'Tell me if I'm hurting.'

'I don't mind a bit of ordinary pain at a time like this. That's not what bothers me. Give me your honest opinion, Colin. Do you really think there's a possibility it's stopped rising?'

'Anything's possible. I'll check again in a little while. Louise, there's something I've been meaning to say. You'll laugh, but I—'

In mid-message, Fletcher's fingers froze. The faintest of tremors beneath them had developed into a shudder. He said sharply, 'Hold on. The stack's slipping.'

There was just time for him to grip Louise by the arms before the subsidence got into its stride. The water, like a thousand frigid footsteps, ran up their bodies and over their heads. He felt Louise struggle. Although he had snatched a breath, it was a shallow one that was doing little to prevent the collapse of his lungs. His glasses came off, drifted away. Removing a hand from her, he struck out desperately, felt his mouth break surface for a tantalizing instant before it submerged once more, cheating him of replenishment. Thrusting with both legs, he caught a projection with his left foot and obtained lift-off, bobbed clear again of the water, stayed there long enough to suck in air.

Louise had risen with him. Adapting his grip, he turned on to his back and began to tow her.

Choking noises came from her nose and throat. Legs pistoning, he kept up sufficient momentum to keep them afloat while she coughed and heaved, fighting for breath. Painfully, his head struck a wall. He twisted into a new course.

Half a dozen improvised strokes carried them both the width of the storeroom to the further wall. This time the impact was more damaging. Something outcropping and metallic jagged his scalp. Clawing blindly, he located it with a couple of fingers and held on. It felt like one of the hooks from which the tools had been suspended. It was attached firmly to the wall: by wedging his forearm across it, he was able to lift Louise by the waist until her head and neck were clear of the water and she could splutter with impunity. The level was just up to his chin, caressing him spasmodically.

His body had ceased to feel the cold. It drifted insensitively beneath, barely a part of him, occasionally bumping lightly against the brickwork. After a while, Louise dragged in a long, tortured breath and expelled it with a moan.

'Take it easy,' he advised.

'Tell that . . . to your grandmother.' She panted, coughed twice more, sagged against him. 'I thought we'd both had it. What happened to the sacks?'

'Let us down properly, I'm afraid. You were right, I shouldn't have moved. But I've a good grip on a wall bracket. Hang on tight.'

'Don't worry. I'm the dependent little woman.' She gave a brief laugh which ended in a coughing bout. When it was over, she clasped arms about his neck.

Fletcher tried to ignore the chewing pain in his arm. Trapped inside the hook, the muscle was threatening to cramp, screaming for release. To disengage his mind, he began monitoring the progress of the tide-level. With the slight fluctuations that were taking place, it was hard to tell whether it was remaining constant or actually doing what it felt as if it were doing, which was creeping slowly and inexorably towards his earlobes. If he could have spared an arm, he would have explored above his head to measure its distance from the ceiling. The impression he had was that the plaster was exceedingly close, and eager to narrow the gap. Why, he thought dully, am I clinging on? What's the use?

Louise's voice blew breath into his ear. 'Is this getting us somewhere?'

'It's keeping us static, I hope.'

'How long can we stay like this?'

'First one down to the floor's a sissy.'

'I used to be able to hold my breath for forty seconds. If you want me to find out how I've worn over the years, let me know.'

'Could you loosen your arms just a little? I'm getting noises in the ears.'

The pressure slackened. He blinked, shook his head. 'That's funny,' Louise said presently. 'I've got them now.'

'Got what?'

'Noises. Are yours sort of high-pitched, like wailing banshees?'

'Sort of. But that's only natural, when you consider . . .' Fletcher gave his head another shake. 'They're getting louder. Must be the immersion effect. If I didn't know better, I'd swear it was a car siren.'

The first action of the crew from the leading car was to turn off the hydrant. While they did that, the sergeant in charge ran for the main entrance of the farmhouse. It swung open at a touch. The hall light had been left on, showing him an open door at the rear end. It led into a kitchen, across which snaked a two-inch diameter hosepipe from an open window to a door in the corner, fastened back to expose the top of a flight of steps.

From the nozzle of the hose a trickle of water continued to emerge, adding itself to the subterranean pool that had formed to the level of the third step down. Glaring at it, the sergeant swore explicitly.

'Sarge . . .' A constable tramped in from the hall. 'We've got a hook-up with D.I. Cummings in his car—he's on his way here with the owner. He says there's another outlet from the storeroom.'

'Where?'

'In the yard. There's a manhole next to the house. The access has been blocked off, but if we lift the cover—'

'Let's get out there.' With lumbering haste the sergeant led the way, pausing to wrench from the kitchen wall a heavy brass poker attached by a chain to hooks. 'Grab any other tools you can find,' he directed, striding across flagstones to the exterior corner of the farmhouse. 'And get those headlamps focused over here.'

A flashlight was produced. With its aid, the sergeant

located a steel manhole cover alongside the wallbase and gave it an experimental thump with the poker. It jumped a little, disturbing grime. Kneeling, he inserted the brass tip into the corroded ring at one end, formed a fulcrum with his kneecap, heaved lustily. The edge of the cover lifted an inch, clashed down again. Another of the team darted into position.

'Try it again, Sarge.'

As the edge rose a second time, he inserted fingers and thrust the metal upwards. The cavity beneath was earth-filled and pungent. Stooping, the sergeant emitted a bellow. 'Anyone down there?'

A faint answering cry floated up.

'Bloody hell,' said the sergeant's colleague. 'Someone's alive, at any rate.'

'Anyone found a shovel?'

Outhouse doors were being opened and slammed. Containing his impatience, the sergeant waited until a constable ran across to hand him something which he eyed with near-incredulity. 'This the best we can do? On a farm?'

'We'll keep looking,' the man said, hurt.

'Do that.' The sergeant set to work with the implement, the size of a beach-spade, its haft snapped off near the grip. Evil-smelling though it was, the soil inside the manhole was moist and soft: in moments he was two feet down and having to operate one-handed. The blade hit something solid. Discarding the tool, he lay full-length and put his head into the space. 'Can you hear me, down there?'

'We hear you.' The voice was startlingly close. 'You sound a little to one side of us. If you want to knock a way through, go ahead.'

The sergeant grinned up at his men. 'What do you say, fellahs? Shall we keep going, just to please 'em?'

★

A split-second after the initial thud, something hit the water and sank. Instantly there was a shaft of feeble light. It looked artificial. Further thumps followed, sending more fragments into the depths. The light increased. Synthetic or not, it held out hope, promise. With his free arm, Fletcher gave Louise an encouraging hoist.

'You first,' he said. 'I'm getting a little tired of supporting you.'

CHAPTER 17

'That'll do for now.' Detective-Inspector Cummings signalled to his assistant. 'Until I've taken a further statement from your wife—your ex, I'm sorry—there's not much point in our trying to tie up every loose end. We've got Deedes remanded for a week, so there's time enough. Feeling fitter after your kip?'

'Apart from knotted sinew.' Fletcher caressed his right biceps. 'If it weren't for Louise, I'd have walked out of here first thing this morning. But they seem to want her in for another night, at least. So I decided to play the invalid and stop on too.'

'All on the National Health.' Cummings ran an appraising eye over the prevailing pastel green of the hospital room. 'You could do worse . . . especially as you've no home to go to. The cottage, I'm afraid, is a write-off. Even if it weren't, I doubt if—'

'You're right, I wouldn't.' Fletcher hesitated over his next words. 'I want to thank you, Inspector, for all you did. Including the cottage episode. I understand you risked your life.'

'It was damn hot,' admitted the inspector. 'And a wasted effort, into the bargain. Sad about Mrs Maynard.

Not balanced, was she? Obviously this idea of a family of her own had become an obsession. If she couldn't have the kids, nobody else was going to.'

'So there's no doubt in your mind she deliberately set fire to the place?'

'Is there any in yours?'

'Not much. I know, now, what kind of a woman she was.'

'There are more of them about,' said Cummings sagely, 'than you might think possible. In extreme cases they'll do anything, literally anything, to achieve what they so desperately want, and if they still don't make it . . . Try not to condemn her, is my advice. She wasn't in her right mind.'

'I don't condemn her. I blame myself.' Refastening his dressing-gown, Fletcher moved restlessly to the window. 'I wonder,' he murmured, gazing out at other buildings, 'what she really hoped to gain?'

'A few days, probably. Maybe, with luck, several weeks. By the time your bodies were discovered, she may have reckoned on being out of the country with the children and perhaps that dominated brother of hers, and his daughter. A cosy little family set-up in South America or some such place.'

Fletcher turned with a frown. 'Did I understand you to say that you allowed Jock Deedes to make a call to her at the cottage?'

'I let him use the phone,' corrected the inspector. 'He made out he wanted to speak to his lawyer. But I figured there was a chance he'd try to get in touch with his sister, to warn her off—which is just what he did. So I watched him dial and got the number, then broke the connection before it could ring. After that I had to wait while we persuaded British Telecom to part with the address.'

'You think that delay might have had something to do with Eva's brainstorm?'

Cummings looked dubious. 'Maybe she was expecting

him to call, you mean, with details of some arrangement? And when he didn't, she panicked? In her mental state, anything's feasible. But we can't totally rule out an accident. Was Mrs Maynard a smoker?'

'On occasion, under stress.'

'There you are, then. She could easily have been puffing away on the bed and set fire to the sheets. We'll know more when we get the fire officer's report.'

'Whether it was by accident or design,' Fletcher said bluntly, returning from the window, 'is fairly irrelevant, wouldn't you say? One way or another, she was heading for a fall. I'm just thankful the children were able to get out safely. Did Miss Wentworth sound harassed when she rang you this morning?'

Musingly, the inspector shook his head. 'She sounded as if she was rather enjoying herself.'

'All the same,' remarked Fletcher, flexing his arm, 'she must be wondering what's hit her. A forcible dose of surrogate motherhood can't come as anything but a shock, even if it's just for the night. We'll have to find some way of thanking her. If she hadn't taken the trouble to call you last night . . .'

'Ferrari, too,' Cummings reminded him.

'Yes, I misjudged him. He's less of a muddler than I thought.'

'But for him, you could still have been drifting around that cellar, the pair of you. By itself, I doubt if Miss Wentworth's call would have rung alarm bells to that extent.'

'I'll slip him an extra bonus. Eva thought he was . . .' Fletcher stopped, pondered for a moment. 'I see it now,' he said quietly. 'She was bound to denigrate him, of course. She wanted him out of the way, to leave herself and Jock a clear field. What a cretin I've been.'

'You weren't to know she was mentally over the top. Since last night, incidentally, that brother of hers has simply fallen apart. The moment he knew she was dead, he seemed to stop trying, told us all we wanted to know. She must have had some kind of sibling hold over him.'

'Exactly the impression I got. But I think, too,' added Fletcher, 'he was nursing a genuine grievance about the whole question of child custody. As a parent, he'd suffered himself. Obviously he saw it as a crusade he was fighting on behalf of his sister.'

'Heaven protect us from the crusaders.'

'What's happening about that daughter of his—Hilary?'

'If he goes to gaol—as he will, for attempted murder—she'll have to be taken into care.'

Fletcher pondered again. 'We'll see about that,' he said eventually. 'And talking of prison sentences . . . what's the position regarding Louise? Presumably there'll be some technical charge against her over this other guy, the one she dealt with in the attic. Has she remembered yet?'

'I did put a question to her about him,' Cummings said cautiously. 'She replied, *Oh, you mean the one who kept bringing me horrible little meals.* Then her face went sort of blank and she kept quiet. I think something might have just come back to her, only muddled. I didn't pursue it.'

'She'll have to know.'

'Sure, but it'll keep. Let her adjust. She'll be up for unlawful killing, no doubt, but in view of all the circumstances . . . If it were anything other than a suspended sentence, or less, I'd be a very surprised detective.'

'Meanwhile,' Fletcher said bitterly, 'Culprit number three, the inscrutable Rosenberg, rides off into the sunset without a scratch. Any chance of catching up with him?'

'Depends what more we can worm out of Deedes in the next day or so. Knowing his real identity doesn't mean that we're home and dry. He's had his marching orders and gone off—who knows where? From all accounts, he's a drifter anyway. They can be the devil to nail.'

'And on top of that,' Fletcher added with a wry glance at the inspector's assistant, a slim constable who had been waiting patiently and in silence near the door since the end of the official interrogation, 'he has enough charm, I imagine, to talk his way into or out of anything. If he hadn't, none of this would have happened.'

'Who knows?' The inspector rose creakily from his NHS-issue, tubular steel, padded plastic chair. 'I must get back to my patch. You and your domestic problems, Mr Fletcher, interrupted a precisely-planned itinerary, did you know that? Don't apologize, if you were intending to. It was a nice little challenge. 'Bye for now, sir. I'll be in touch.'

The staff nurse pivoted in her tracks, looking severe. 'This is the female section. Were you looking for somebody?'

'Mrs Colin Fletcher?'

'You'll find Mrs *Louise* Fletcher in that side ward, third door along. She's rather tired still, so keep it short. Are you the husband?'

'No,' he said. 'No relation.'

From a tilted position against pillows, Louise opened her eyes, locked on to him, blinked, raised her eyebrows. 'Enter the walking wounded. How did you escape? They won't let me out of bed.'

He sat on the mattress-edge. 'Evidently I'm judged to be still in with a chance. How's the double pneumonia?'

'Closing ranks. I'm pumped so full of vaccines, I feel as if I'm adrift in mid-air. Can't grab hold of my brain . . . I want you to tell me something. That man. The one in the attic, the one I dreamt about. The inspector was asking questions. I couldn't remember, but I've been thinking it over and I believe I—'

Without premeditation, Fletcher interrupted her. 'You

dealt with him quite decisively, I'm glad to say. Nothing to worry about there.'

'What does that mean?'

'He asked for what he got. Any woman would have done the same.'

'Are you saying that I . . . ?'

'There'll be a technical charge against you,' he explained, plunging heavily. 'A token penalty, that's all. Once it's been dealt with you can forget it. Legally or morally, you can't be blamed.'

'You make it sound like an accounting oversight.' Louise stared blindly ahead. 'I can't shove it out of my mind as easily as that.'

'Think of the children,' he urged. 'You want to see them, don't you?'

For a moment he thought his words had evaporated into thin air. Then he saw her eyes regain focus. She rose slightly from the pillow. 'Are they here?' she demanded.

'Not yet. Your chum Sally Wentworth is bringing them along later this afternoon. They spent what was left of the night with her, apparently.'

'At the bungalow? Poor old Mrs Wentworth. She's supposed to have peace and quiet.'

'I doubt if either of them were in a mood to disturb her rest.' Fletcher fingered the bed coverlet.

Louise's survey wandered off about the room before returning to him. 'You've lost the cottage, I hear. What do you plan to do?'

'Find a hotel, while I sort myself out.'

'There's a spare bed at the house. I assume there's still a house. That hasn't been burnt down or flooded, has it?'

'Not as far as I know. But you won't want me intruding. I'll try The George in Bancester.'

'You wouldn't be in the way. To tell you the honest truth . . .'

'Well, go ahead. Tell me.'

'I'd be quite glad to have somebody around.'

'Always happy to oblige,' he said lightly. 'But for how long?'

'Indefinitely, if you like. There's no rush.'

Fletcher devoted time and concentration to the flicking of imaginary specks off the coverlet. 'That's very good of you. I'll stay for a night or two, if I may.'

'No trouble,' said Louise, with equal formality. 'Breakfast at seven-thirty? You can have it with the children.'

'That'll be fine.'

The silence that settled between them was of the dead-weight immovable variety, proof against the forces immediately available to shift it. Outside, a trolley rumbled down the corridor to an accompaniment of tinkling china. The heat of the ward was awesome. Louise lay in a sleeveless hospital smock that failed to hide some incipient bruising above her right elbow, scratches across both shoulders. The scratches had been smeared with something transparent. A light dressing covered part of one side of her face.

With a tangible effort she said, 'Those glasses aren't your own, are they?'

He touched them self-consciously. 'I borrowed them from one of the male nurses. They suit me quite well.'

'When we get home . . .'

Hearing voices outside, Louise paused. A head appeared round the door. 'May we come in? We're a bit early, but they said it would be all right.'

'Sal, how lovely to see you. Are the children . . . ?'

The door opened wider. 'In you come, you two. Your mum can't wait to say hello.'

Sally stood aside to make room. With some hesitancy, Kevin and Terri made their entry, the girl first: both were clad in bright blue anoraks, and against Terri's left hip hung a multi-coloured purse on a shoulder-strap.

Advancing to within a foot or two of the bed, they stood regarding their mother a little doubtfully. Louise swallowed, and produced a wide smile. 'Hi, loves,' she said shakily. 'Got a kiss for the invalid?'

Terri threw herself on to the bed, to be consumed by an embrace. More reservedly, Kevin pursued her, sustaining his older-brother dignity for a few brief seconds before succumbing to the pressure. Fletcher and Sally exchanged smiles. She said, 'They've both been extremely good. A couple of treasures.'

Holding them off, Louise examined them critically. 'So you managed not to reduce your Auntie Sal or her mother to a jelly. Kept yourselves washed and brushed up, I hope? You look passable.'

'Mummy . . .' Terri spoke on a high note of interest. 'Why are you talking like that?'

'Lost a couple of teeth. Look.' She bared her gums.

'Did you trip over?'

'I suppose I did, in a way. How did you get here?' Louise asked Sally over their heads. 'Not by train?'

'No, I hired a car. It was really the only way.'

'Send the bill to us. You know, Sal, we're truly most terribly grateful. I don't know how we can—'

'It's been an experience, believe me. I've never come up against police inquiries before. Mother was agog.'

'Kevin, Terri . . . have you thanked Auntie Sal for having you?'

'Yes, they did. Very nicely.'

'Let me hear you say it again.'

Terri peeped up from the nest she had established next to the pillows. 'Thank you for letting us stay with you, Auntie Sal.'

'It's been a pleasure, dear.'

'We were staying with Eva,' Terri informed her mother. 'Only there was a fire.'

'I know, darling.' Louise sent Fletcher a wary glance. 'I

heard about it. Thank goodness you were able to get away.'

'Eva didn't. She—'

'No, she wasn't so lucky. There it is: it can't be helped. I want you to tell me how you've been getting on, the pair of you. About today, for instance. Did you eat a good lunch?'

'Me and Kevin went into the garden, but Eva stayed behind. It was *awf'ly* hot,' Terri announced, saucer-eyed. 'You could feel how hot it was, right from where we were standing.'

Responding to Louise's helpless look, Fletcher said on a practical key, 'Goes to show, doesn't it? Fire's a dangerous thing. Never treat it carelessly.'

While Terri was considering this, Kevin put a question. 'Are you coming home today, Mum?'

'Tomorrow, I believe.' His face fell. 'But your father,' she added quickly, 'is going back with you. You'll be able to sleep in your own bedroom tonight, give your Auntie Sal a break.'

'Is Dad staying?'

'For a while, at least. You'd like that?'

'I've got some drawings to show him,' said the boy, and did a handspring across the bed.

'Well done, you two,' Sally murmured.

Terri emerged from her trance. 'Eva *would* have got out,' she confided to her mother, 'only her door wouldn't open.'

'And her bedroom window was too small,' explained Kevin from the bedside locker, 'for her to climb out of.'

Fletcher took a bold decision. Better, he had once heard or read, for children to talk out a traumatic experience than to bottle it up. 'Why,' he asked, matter-of-factly, 'wouldn't the door open? Did it jam?'

Terri shook an emphatic head, disturbing her ringlets. 'It was locked.'

'Couldn't she unlock it?'

'It was locked from the outside.' Unzipping the Technicolor purse, she delved within, produced a heavy key which she placed with care on the coverlet. Alongside it she deposited a box of matches, decoratively emblazoned with the head of a unicorn. 'You can have these,' she told her mother generously, zipping up the purse. She gave a sudden chuckle, a gurgle deep in her throat. 'I shan't be needing them any more.'